MW00473288

LEGION
BOOK
SEVEN

LEGION

A.D. STARRLING

COPYRIGHT

FOREWORD

I am darkness.
I am wrath.
I am destruction.
I am oppressor.
I belong to Hell.
~ Drake Hunter

CHAPTER ONE

SERENA BLAKE STOPPED IN FRONT OF THE DOOR, RAISED
a hand, and hesitated.

Heavy silence filtered through from the room on the
other side, the stillness echoed by the oppressive hush
shrouding the LeBlanc estate. Serena knew what awaited
her beyond the door. She steeled herself, rapped her
knuckles on the wood, and called out a warning.

"I'm coming in."

Stale, muggy air washed over her as she crossed the
threshold, carrying with it the faint odor of human sweat.

Artemus Steele's bedroom was dark, the curtains at the
windows pulled closed against the daylight. She navigated
the floor and stopped when her foot knocked against
something. She looked down, the nanorobots in her retinas
adjusting to the dim lighting.

The tray of food Callie had brought that morning lay
untouched, as she'd suspected it would be.

Serena sighed and walked around the bed.

Artemus was a shadow where he sat on the hardwood

floor, his back against the foot of the four poster and his legs stretched out before him. Jacob Schroeder slept with his head on the angel's lap, his body curved into a tight ball and Smokey clutched snugly in his thin arms. The rabbit opened a heavy eye and looked at her blearily before closing it once more.

Artemus continued staring into space, as if he hadn't registered her presence.

"You need to eat."

Her command got no reaction. Serena stayed still for a moment before making a frustrated sound and raking a hand through her hair. As a super soldier, she shouldn't have felt exhausted. Except she did.

She had never experienced the bone-deep tiredness that came with having her heart shattered into a million pieces and sharing that grief with so many others.

"You aren't the only one who lost Drake, Artemus. I did too. And so did everyone else."

Her voice remained steady despite the knot twisting her stomach. She couldn't give in to her emotions. Not again. It wouldn't bring Drake back and it only made Nate feel helpless in the face of her anguish.

Artemus stiffened slightly at her words. Faint lines marred his brow.

"He was my twin," he said stonily. "My blood."

"And he was my lover!" Serena snapped.

"Did you love him?"

His question made her eyes widen and drew a sharp breath from her lips.

Artemus had raised his head and was glaring at her accusingly.

Serena paused and swallowed. She knew it wasn't her he was angry at.

"Yes."

"Did you ever tell him?"

Artemus's words shot through her like bullets tearing into her broken, bleeding heart.

"Yes." Her reply came out a whisper. "Once."

"I never did," Artemus muttered. "It's too late for me to say it now and for you to repeat it."

Anger quickened Serena's pulse at his callous words. She would have closed the distance between them and punched Artemus in the face had it not been for the sleeping child in his arms.

"That's it!" she grated out. "It's been two weeks since we got back from Rome. You need to quit being a mopey asshole and talk to us!"

Serena strode over to the windows, grabbed the edges of the curtains, and pulled them open with a brisk motion. Blinding light flooded the room, exposing the dust motes filling the air and covering the furnishings.

Artemus swore and raised a hand to shield his face. Dark stubble covered his jawline and upper lip and his golden hair was dull and greasy.

Jacob squinted before blinking at the brightness, his face swollen and his eyes red and puffy from crying. He sat up slowly, his expression numb and his arms tightening around the limp rabbit.

Drake wasn't the only one they'd lost in Rome.

Solomon Weiss, Jacob's adoptive father and the fallen archangel Sariel turned demon, had been Jacob's gate. He'd sacrificed himself during their last battle to stop that gate from opening.

Serena hardened herself against the young Guardian's forlorn look.

"The three of you stink," she said in a hard voice. "Go have a shower and come downstairs."

She grabbed the tray of uneaten food and stormed toward the exit.

"Don't wanna," Artemus mumbled, his tone low and petulant.

The rabbit's eyes flashed with a crimson glow of defiance.

Jacob clutched Artemus's arm, his face similarly sullen.

Serena stopped on the threshold and arched an eyebrow at the angel and the Guardians clinging to him. "You either shower and get dressed on your own or we're coming up here to do it for you. It's your choice."

Artemus's outraged snarl followed her out of the bedroom.

"How the hell is that a choice?!"

Serena's mouth stretched in a flinty smile as she navigated the corridors of the mansion. That was the first hint of genuine emotion Artemus had shown since their return from Europe. She sobered as she went downstairs and put the cold food away.

What had happened in the cave deep under the Vatican gardens and the monastery where Artemus and Drake's mothers had once sought refuge was something none of them had gotten over yet.

It was thanks to Jacob's divine beast and Artemus's new sword that they'd managed to defeat the army of nigh-indestructible Nephilim Beelzebub had raised to tear open Jacob's gate and capture Drake. Having thwarted Beelzebub and Samyaza's efforts to drag Drake to Hell, they'd tasted victory for the briefest of moments before everything had been ripped from their grasp.

Belial's appearance had shocked all of them. None more so than Artemus.

Though they knew Ba'al's leader to be one of the most powerful demons in existence, they hadn't anticipated that he'd turn up personally to complete the task his associates had failed to execute.

They would have lost Artemus too that day had Sebastian, Daniel, and Otis not intervened to stop him from following his brother into Hell. But it was Drake who had ultimately saved his twin by cutting off his right wing and forcing him to let go.

Artemus's blood had grown cold and congealed in thick puddles beneath him before they'd managed to drag his body from the edge of the chasm where Drake had disappeared, his voice raw from screaming and his face streaked with tear marks.

He'd fallen into a state of shock shortly after, his body growing cold as ice and his gaze vacant. It was in that condition that they'd maneuvered him onto the private jet that had borne them to Chicago, their senses too raw still from their latest encounter with Ba'al to wish to travel through one of Sebastian's rifts.

The Vatican was still in the midst of dealing with the aftermath of the battle. They'd blamed the destruction the rise of the Nephilim had wreaked on the capital and the Holy See on the earthquakes that had rocked the region that night. So far, the world continued to believe that false claim.

As for the giant sinkhole that now occupied a significant portion of the Vatican gardens, not even Persephone had been able to stop the media from getting their hands on the shocking images of the jagged chasm and broadcasting them to all seven continents.

No one but they and the Vatican agents who had fought beside them knew the borehole was a result of Artemus and Drake bringing down the roof of the cave onto their enemy.

Serena was still frowning when she strolled inside the TV room a short while later. She stopped and studied the figures slouched and draped on various pieces of furniture.

"Seriously, you guys are almost as bad as him."

Callie Stone sniffed. She was huddled next to Nate Conway on the couch, her eyes suspiciously red. Leah Chase bit her lip and glared out at the garden, her gaze glistening and her fingers white around Haruki Kuroda's hand on the window seat.

Daniel Lenton stared blindly at the open bible in his hands where he leaned against the wall beside them, his face miserable. Sebastian Lancaster and Otis Boone were attempting to play a game of chess at a low table to the left without much success.

"Did they eat?" Nate said quietly.

"No. The three of them are being stubborn."

"That is nothing new." A muscle jumped in Sebastian's cheek. "But the child at least should be made to consume some food. He is still young and he used a lot of divine energy during the battle."

"I suspect he might bite us if we try," Serena drawled. "And Smokey will have something to say about it too."

"That pup is too obstinate for his own good," Sebastian grumbled.

Gravel crunched faintly out the front of the mansion.

Serena tensed.

"It's only Elton and Barbara," Haruki murmured. "They said they'd drop by again today."

"There's more than two people out there," Otis said morosely, his gaze on the chess pieces before him.

CHAPTER TWO

SEBASTIAN LOOKED AT THE SERAPH SITTING OPPOSITE him, shoulders drooping. Otis had been more quiet than usual since the appearance of his latest symbols and their return from Rome. He knew the young man was wracked with guilt about what had happened to Artemus.

That all of them would have stopped the angel from following his brother to Hell was no comfort to Otis. He was Artemus's closest friend and no doubt felt he'd betrayed him the most.

No one had spoken about the increased powers the two inverted Vs on his left palm had seemingly gifted him with.

The doorbell rang. When it became clear no one was going to go open it, Sebastian sighed and rose to his feet. He crossed the foyer, his curiosity piqued; he wondered whom it was Otis had sensed.

His eyes widened slightly when he saw the figures gathered on the porch.

"Sorry." Elton LeBlanc made a face where he stood at

the head of the group. "We...bumped into some people who wanted to visit too."

Sebastian couldn't help but feel that 'bumped into' weren't quite the words Elton would have chosen had present company not been within earshot. No one bumped into Akihito Kuroda, the leader of the Kuroda Group, unless they had a death wish. And he was certain the same applied to Ivan Vlašic, the mild-faced Immortal standing beside him.

Barbara Nolan eyed the two men with open curiosity where she stood between them, while Jeremiah Chase and Archbishop Holmes observed the Yakuza boss and the Immortal with carefully guarded expressions.

"We brought sake," Renji Ogawa declared, a faint sheen of sweat on his forehead despite the autumnal breeze blowing across Chicago.

Sebastian suspected the Yakuza bodyguard's strained look had everything to do with the palpable tension coursing through the mismatched party on the porch.

"It's not even lunchtime." Naomi Wagner walked past Ogawa where he stood clutching a case of dark-colored bottles. Her face softened as she stared at Sebastian, a white cat with heterochromatic eyes keeping abreast of her. "Hi."

She rose on tiptoes and kissed him, her blue gaze searching his.

"Hello."

Sebastian swallowed a sigh, aware that he couldn't completely mask the sorrow that had been his companion for the past two weeks. Artemus's pain was a pulsing, crimson band across the bond that linked all the Guardians.

He relaxed at Naomi's touch. There was little he could hide from the woman he intended to marry. Not that he had proposed to her yet.

"It's never too early for alcohol," Isabelle Mueller said brightly. The Immortal assigned to Elton LeBlanc's security detail raised an eyebrow where she lounged against the porch railing. "Besides, I have a feeling you guys could do with getting drunk."

"She's not wrong," Shamus Carmichael murmured.

The head of Elton's security team glanced uneasily at Ogawa and Vlašic, seemingly in need of a stiff drink himself.

"Can we come in?" Vlašic said politely. "There's a rather disturbing chicken peeking at us from the corner of the house."

Gemini the cat meowed uneasily.

"You noticed the fowl too?" Kuroda murmured.

"She has gimlet eyes," the Immortal replied. "They are hard to miss."

"My apologies." Sebastian stood aside and let their guests in before poking his head out the door and casting a narrow-eyed stare at Gertrude, the undead chicken who ruled the grounds of the LeBlanc estate. "Nate fed you two hours ago."

The chicken's gaze flashed. She flapped her wings menacingly.

"I know what you're thinking, but you'd all get food poisoning if you ate her," Naomi said firmly after he'd closed the door.

"Who said anything about eating her afterward?" Sebastian muttered.

Naomi grinned. "I like it when you go all dark on me."

They were about to kiss again when they became aware of a battery of pointed stares.

Sebastian cleared his throat. "This way."

Haruki and Leah brightened when they saw their fathers. Serena startled before striding across the room and embracing Vlašic tightly, Nate rising from the couch to follow suit.

"Archbishop Holmes." Surprise danced across Daniel's face as he came forward to greet the clergyman. "I didn't know you were coming over."

"I was in the country for business," Holmes said with a mild wave of a hand.

Haruki hugged his father. "Did you come straight from the airport?"

The Yakuza boss patted his son's back lightly, relief darkening his eyes. "Yes." He pulled away and stared searchingly at the young man. "I heard what happened from Ogawa. You should have called."

Haruki grimaced. "I didn't want to bother you. I know how busy you are with the group."

"I'm never too busy for you, son." The older Kuroda's warm gaze landed on the girl standing behind Haruki. "You must be Leah."

Leah dipped her chin. "Hi. It's nice to meet you, Mr. Kuroda."

The Yakuza boss's expression turned appraising. "It's nice to meet you too." He glanced at Jeremiah. "I believe your father is a Chicago PD detective."

Leah's eyes widened slightly at his cool tone. "Hmm. Yes, he is."

Haruki's expression became strained. Sebastian suspected the Yakuza heir knew this confrontation had been on the cards ever since he and Leah had started dating.

Jeremiah frowned at Haruki's father.

The air temperature in the room dropped by a couple of degrees.

"Now would be the right time for someone to crack a joke," Isabelle hissed to Shamus out of the corner of her mouth.

"What kinda joke?"

"A cop, a Yakuza, a bishop, an Immortal, and a witch walk into a bar—*ouch!*"

"I apologize for my companions," Elton said stiffly, eyeballing the Immortal bodyguard Shamus had sent stumbling across the floor, courtesy of the elbow he'd shoved in her side.

Barbara sighed heavily. "Alright, now that everybody's tried to show who's the biggest cock in the roost, can we get on with our business?"

Leah sucked in air. Elton flushed. Holmes murmured an apology to the Lord. Jeremiah pinched the bridge of his nose. Vlašic looked amused. Kuroda's lips twitched before he put on his best stony expression, a trace of admiration darting across his face as he gazed at the older witch.

"I can't believe she just said that," Callie murmured.

Naomi rolled her eyes. "I can."

"Where's Artemus?" Elton said.

"Still holed up in his room." A frown clouded Serena's face as she glanced at the clock above the mantelpiece. "Speaking of which, it's been twenty minutes. I told him we'd come and personally drag them into the shower if he didn't get himself and the other two cleaned up and down here."

Barbara grimaced. "They still haven't bathed?"

"Nope. It's starting to smell mighty fusty in that room."

"Maybe we should hose them down in the garden," Isabelle suggested.

"You're just saying that 'cause you want to see Artemus naked," Shamus chided. "You already have Mark."

"Doesn't mean I can't look," the Immortal said defensively.

Elton headed for the exit. "I'll go talk to him."

"I'll come with you," Barbara said grimly. "They're having that shower, whether they like it or not."

Elton stopped in his tracks. "They are?"

"Yes."

"I'll make us something to eat," Nate said.

"I'll help," Callie murmured.

A shout echoed from upstairs a moment later.

"Hey!" Artemus yelled in the distance. "What the hell do you think you're doing?! *Hands off my pants, lady!*"

Jacob's similarly outraged, boyish screech and the hellhound's ferocious snarl followed.

Isabelle grinned. "Ten bucks says someone loses a finger."

Jeremiah frowned at her.

The Immortal shrugged. "What? I'm just trying to lighten the morbid mood."

CHAPTER THREE

"ARE THEY GONNA BE OKAY?" VLAŠIC SAID WARILY.

"Yeah. They're all bark and no bite." Serena gazed curiously at the Immortal she and Nate considered their father. "What brings you here?"

Vlašic arched an eyebrow. "Am I not allowed to visit my children?"

Serena sighed. "You are. But that's not really why you're here, is it?"

Vlašic stayed silent.

Suspicion dawned in Serena's mind. "Is it the Immortal societies? Did we do something in Rome to upset them in some way?"

Though Vlašic didn't reply, she could tell from his guarded expression that she'd just touched a nerve. The first thread of unease filtered through her.

Nate and Callie returned with a butler's trolley full of sandwiches and hot and cold drinks. Sebastian had just poured tea for Naomi and Holmes when heavy footsteps stomped down the mansion's main staircase. Artemus stormed into the TV room and rocked to a halt.

He glared at everyone before focusing his scowl on the food. "What is this, a bloody tea party?!"

"And good afternoon to you too, Mr. Grumpy," Callie said drily.

A sulking Jacob and Smokey trailed in Artemus's wake, the hellhound still growling faintly as he hopped alongside the others in his rabbit form. The growling stopped when he saw Gemini. A repentant huff left him as the white cat darted over and greeted him with a head bump.

To Serena's relief, Artemus and Jacob were dressed in a fresh change of clothes and no longer smelled like yesterday's garbage. A band-aid covered a nick on the angel's freshly shaven jawline.

"I thought witches were supposed to have a steady hand," Artemus grumbled at Barbara as she and Elton came in behind him, their clothes dotted with damp patches.

"It was a deliberate slip of the fingers," the High Priestess of the Chicago Coven said icily. "That was the only way to shut you up and get you to sit still. Be thankful it wasn't your neck."

Serena bit back a smile.

"Oooh, that's vicious," Isabelle said. "I *like* it."

Kuroda looked like he approved too.

Someone's stomach rumbled loudly in the silence. Everyone stared at the hellhound. Smokey twitched before glancing at Artemus.

The angel sighed. "Go on. I'm not stopping you from eating."

Smokey rubbed his nose sheepishly with his paws and

headed over to the food trolley. Jacob hesitated before going after him.

Callie narrowed her eyes at Artemus. "You need to eat too."

"I'm not hungry," he retorted.

Serena swallowed a sigh. The way Artemus's gaze kept darting to a beef sandwich said otherwise.

"Look, kid, unless you want me to pry your jaws open with magic and shove that sandwich down your throat, I suggest you do as the Chimera says," Barbara threatened in a steely voice.

"I really like her," Kuroda told Haruki.

"Dear God," Jeremiah muttered to no one in particular.

Leah nudged her father sharply with an elbow.

Jacob sneezed as some mustard went down the wrong way. He squinted, his eyes watering. "I'm sorry."

"It's alright." Callie passed him a tissue. "Go on, blow your nose."

The young Guardian did as he was told and reached for a second sandwich before crawling onto Callie's lap. Callie's face softened as she closed an arm around him.

It was a while before Holmes and Vlašic finally voiced their reasons for coming to Chicago.

Holmes set down his empty teacup, his expression somber. "As you can probably guess, Drake falling into the hands of Hell is something none of us wanted to see happen."

They'd all finished eating bar for Smokey, who sounded like he was inhaling bacon where he and Gemini lay under the couch.

Artemus frowned. "Except for Samyaza."

Holmes dipped his chin gravely. "Except for Drake's father, yes."

Serena's unease turned to full-blown dread when she saw the clergyman glance at her father.

Vlašic took his cue and studied Artemus steadily. "Following the latest incident in Rome, the Vatican organization tasked with hunting out Ba'al reached out formally to the United Nations and the Immortal societies for assistance."

A tense hush descended around them.

"What do you mean?" Serena said slowly. "What kind of assistance?"

"As we speak, the Vatican organization's highest council and that of the United Nations privy to the existence of the Immortals and the divine Guardians are having a joint video conference to decide Artemus and Smokey's fate. A select few Immortals are also attending the meeting by proxy."

The tension swirling through the room thickened.

"And what the hell does that mean, exactly?" Artemus asked in a deadly voice.

Serena wasn't surprised that Vlašic appeared unfazed by the angel's hostile tone. Her adoptive father had seen far worse than a pissed-off divine being in his centuries of existence.

"It means they will be voting on whether to declare the two of you the most highly prized weapons in the world right now." Vlašic exchanged a glance with Holmes. "We are here to lay out the groundwork of what will happen if they reach that decision."

"Which will be what?" Sebastian said stiffly.

"If the world decides Artemus and Smokey must be

protected at all costs, then the archbishop and I are to escort them to a secure facility managed by the U.S. army and the Immortals."

Serena flinched. Nate frowned. Artemus froze.

A dangerous stillness oozed from beneath the couch.

Vlašic sighed in the face of Serena and Nate's expressions. "It's not that kind of facility. No one is going to experiment on them. The aim is to keep them safe."

Serena clenched her teeth, conscious of the thread of anger humming across the Guardians' bond from Artemus and Smokey. Neither she nor Nate had told Artemus and the others that they could now faintly sense the divine ties that linked them. They'd picked up on it after their last battle with Ba'al.

"If they are having to vote on it, I take it some people have already objected to this plan of action?" she said coolly.

Vlašic dipped his head. "Yes. Persephone, Archbishop Holmes, Victor Dvorsky, myself, and a number of other Immortals think it's a terrible idea."

"King said it was asinine," Holmes murmured.

"Asinine is a tame word for what she actually said," Vlašic drawled.

Holmes sighed.

"Alexa is in on this?" Serena asked sharply.

"So is Conrad Greene," Vlašic said calmly. "You know how powerful their family's standing is in the Immortal societies."

Serena chewed her lip. She was glad Vlašic, Dvorsky, and the Immortals who had saved the super soldier children in Greenland were on their side. Still, it didn't take away from the fact that the majority of the Vatican organization and the U.N. would likely vote to effectively imprison Artemus and Smokey.

Elton scowled as he looked from the Immortal to the archbishop. "If the two of you opposed this, then why are you here?"

Though Elton was a member of the same Vatican organization as Holmes, he'd clearly not been kept in the loop and he didn't look happy about that fact.

Serena frowned. *Nor will he exactly be thrilled about his superiors deciding to put Artemus and Smokey in a gilded cage.*

"I agree with Elton," Isabelle said shrewdly as she studied the pair. "You two are too high up on the power ladder to serve as escorts."

Vlašic and Holmes shared another cautious glance.

Barbara's expression cleared. "Oh. I see."

Leah stared at her grandmother. "What?"

The answer came to Serena at the same time Naomi gave voice to it.

"It's to make sure nobody gets any stupid ideas about using Artemus and Smokey for their own gains when they are in the custody of the world's governments," the younger witch murmured with a frown.

"Shit." Jeremiah paled. "Thanks for the nightmares."

Lines furrowed Isabelle's brow. "You're right. It would be like handing over the planet's most deadly nuclear arsenal to a bunch of power-hungry kids notorious for squabbling among themselves."

"You all appear to be forgetting something," Artemus said icily. "What if Smokey and I refuse?"

His question hung in the air for a timeless moment.

"They can't refuse, can they?" Daniel said, his tone hardening.

Otis frowned, as did every Guardian in the room.

"Since this would be for the sake of the entire world, the councils presumed Artemus and Smokey would have no grounds to object to their decision," Vlašic confirmed with a sigh.

"The entire world was oblivious when I lost my brother to demons, so they can piss the hell off!" Artemus growled, his every word dripping with contempt. "Besides, you can't keep me or Smokey safe. Your defenses are futile in the face of Hell's forces."

"Be that as it may," Vlašic said quietly. "We have been granted permission to utilize force if necessary."

Anger sparked across the air as the Guardians reacted to that claim.

Artemus jumped to his feet, his face reddening with rage. "Oh, I would love to see you try!"

Barbara rose and laid a hand on his shoulder. "Calm down."

Artemus clenched and unclenched his fists, seemingly oblivious to the golden armor that now covered his body and the single white wing flaring at his back, his divine powers making everyone's ears ring and the room tremble.

Callie gasped as the couch heaved under her and Jacob. Smokey crawled out from beneath it in his dark hellhound mode, his eyes glowing gold-crimson and a threatening sound rumbling from his powerful throat. He joined Artemus and turned to glare at Vlašic.

The Immortal grimaced and rubbed the back of his neck. "I didn't say *I* would use force."

"If they do come to that decision, then you can tell the Vatican organization and the U.N. to shove it!" Artemus bit out. "Besides, we're gonna be too busy to pander to their high and mighty orders in the coming days."

Serena shared a surprised look with Nate. She could feel the dim, red thread of Artemus's anger fading to gold where it linked the Guardians.

There was only one emotion she sensed from the angel now. Hope.

It made her mouth dry and sent her pulse racing.

Elton gazed at Artemus, puzzled. "Why? What are you going to be doing?"

Artemus shifted back to his human form.

"There's something I didn't tell you." He hesitated as he met their curious stares. "Something Drake told me when he was falling to Hell. It's all I've been able to think about for the past two weeks. I thought I'd imagined it at first, but I'm more certain than ever now that he *did* say those words to me."

"What?!" Serena mumbled hoarsely in the stunned silence, her heart thundering in her chest and her shock echoed by everyone else in the room.

Callie climbed to her feet, her eyes blazing. "What did Drake say?"

Jacob clutched her hand, his expression as fierce as those of the other Guardians in the room.

Artemus took a shaky breath. "He said...*Find me.*'"

CHAPTER FOUR

PERSEPHONE STRUGGLED TO KEEP HER EXPRESSION composed as the Vatican organization's highest body and the U.N. Special Security Council announced their final vote.

"Now that the majority consensus has dictated the primary outcome of this meeting, we must move to the agenda of how to secure Artemus Steele and the beast known as Smokey," the president of the assembly said gravely. "I believe the United States already has a facility in mind supported by the Immortals?"

The U.S. government representative and Victor Dvorsky nodded. Persephone could tell the Immortal was displeased despite his neutral countenance. She muted the rest of the video conference as the president of the assembly requested details of the installation where they were proposing to keep Artemus and Smokey prisoners indefinitely.

Idiots.

Persephone sighed before promptly begging God for

forgiveness. She downed her cooling coffee, speed-dialed another number, and drummed her fingers on her desk while she waited for the call to be answered.

Daniel's voice sounded subdued when he came on the line. "Persephone?"

Persephone frowned. "I take it from your tone that Vlašic and Holmes have put you in the loop about today's special summit?"

"Yes." Daniel's tone hardened. "Has a decision been reached?"

Persephone fisted her hands. "It's not in Artemus and Smokey's favor."

Daniel swore under his breath.

Persephone allowed him the blasphemy and listened silently as he shared the outcome of the meeting with those gathered at the LeBlanc estate. To her surprise, there were no violent outbursts. The rumble of voices behind the priest resumed again with an intensity that spoke of deep focus.

She raised an eyebrow. "I thought Artemus would be raging. Is he still in shock?"

"Oh, he raged alright when he first heard about it. It's the rest of us who are in shock."

Persephone stared at her phone. "What do you mean?"

"Drake told Artemus to come find him in Hell."

Persephone froze. Even Daniel's usual bluntness couldn't detract from the bombshell he'd just dropped.

"What?!" she mumbled numbly.

"That was the last thing Drake told Artemus when Belial dragged him into the Underworld," Daniel said stiffly.

Persephone gazed blindly into space, her mind reeling. "That's—"

"I know." Daniel sighed heavily. "We're just having a discussion about how to proceed."

Persephone almost fell out of her seat. "*What?!*"

Her shout echoed around the pontiff's office and had a Vatican guard poking a head through the door.

"Everything okay, your excellency?"

"Yes." Persephone waited until the man had closed the door before hissing, "*Have you guys lost your minds?!*" into the phone. "How the devil do you think you're going to get into Hell and save Drake? Or even find a way into the Underworld in the first place?!"

"The seventh gate."

Persephone's breath locked in her throat.

"Solomon said only Satanael knows its location, but Artemus thinks we can find it," Daniel stated with grim confidence.

"The gate of the prophesized Apocalypse?" Persephone's knuckles whitened on the desk. "Artemus wants to bring about the End of Days to save his brother? *Is he insane?!*"

"Don't shout," Daniel chided. "It's bad for your blood pressure."

"This job is bad for my blood pressure!" Persephone said between gritted teeth.

A heavy sigh traveled along the line. "He's not intending to bring about the End of Days, Persephone. He's just gonna, well...sneak into Hell, grab Drake, and sneak out again."

Persephone started silently counting to ten.

"Perse? You still there?" Daniel said anxiously.

"Yes," Persephone grated out. "I think you should have Artemus checked out by a doctor. He's clearly delirious. As are the rest of you if you're thinking of going along with this foolish plan."

"Hey!" Artemus yelled in the backdrop. "*I heard that!*"

"Keep your ears to yourself, you stupid angel!" Persephone barked.

"She's not wrong. This is by far the dumbest idea you've ever had," Serena said in the distance.

"Artemus wouldn't know how to sneak into anywhere without causing an uproar," Persephone argued with Daniel. "That guy is like the bull in the proverbial China shop."

"He won't be alone. Smokey, Sebastian, and Callie will go with him."

Persephone's stomach sank.

"You're really serious about this, aren't you?" she said after a short silence.

"Yes." Daniel faltered. "Look, I know it sounds crazy. And I know the odds are stacked against us. But I believe in what we can do, together."

Persephone pinched the bridge of her nose. "You guys are going to go ahead with this cockamamie scheme regardless of what everyone else thinks, aren't you?"

"Yes," came the quiet confirmation.

Persephone scowled. "I cannot in all honesty give you my blessing, Daniel. Not when it means you and the other Guardians and our allies might get hurt. But I won't oppose you either."

"Thank you," Daniel murmured gratefully.

"There's something all of you seem to be forgetting, though," Persephone added in a steely voice. "Artemus is missing a wing. He won't be able to fight at full power without it."

"He has a plan for that too."

VICTOR DVORSKY WALKED INTO ONE OF THE UNITED Nations' cafes, a scowl on his face and his bodyguards trailing in his wake.

It was past one p.m. and most of the lunch crowd had dispersed. Still, Dvorsky suspected the table he was headed for would have remained an oasis of silence in a sea of noise even if the place had been packed. He signaled to his guards to hang back and took a seat between Alexa King and Conrad Greene.

"I take it from your expression that things went like we suspected they would?" King drawled.

Dvorsky eyed the sai dagger spinning on the knuckles of her right hand.

"How did you even get that past security?" he grunted.

King flashed her teeth at him. "I have means."

"I hope it didn't involve killing anyone," Dvorsky retorted.

"Have some faith, Victor," Conrad Greene muttered where he slouched in his chair. "You know I would have stopped her if she'd tried."

King arched an eyebrow. "Oh, really? Last time I checked, I beat you a hundred to seventy-five."

"Seventy-six," Greene said.

King narrowed her eyes. "That fight doesn't count. Rocky jumped into the ring and got in my way."

There was movement under the table. A dog poked his

head out next to King's left thigh, his eyes bright and his ears perking up at the sound of his name.

Dvorksy scowled at the German Shepherd mongrel. "How the hell did you get *him* past security?"

Greene indicated the young woman who sat opposite them. She was staring out at the sunlit river beyond the glass walls, her face serene and her blue eyes focused on something none of them could see.

King lifted some french fries from her plate and fed them to the dog as they all waited for her to speak. Rocky inhaled the offering, licked his chops, and stared at the rest of the fries, a hopeful whine rumbling up his throat.

"The Vatican and the U.N. Special Security Council's decision will come to nothing," the woman finally said, her tone quiet and steady.

"They intend to send a team of special operatives to secure Artemus and Smokey if those two offer up any kind of resistance." Dvorsky paused. "They've asked for our best Immortal agents and super soldiers."

King narrowed her eyes. "Well, I for one sure as hell won't be joining that party."

"Neither will I." Greene frowned. "Nor will any former member of my troops. Laura will have their guts for garters if they do."

Dvorsky blew out a heavy sigh. He knew nothing but an act of God would change King and Greene's minds.

Even then, I suspect they'd have some words with God.

The woman opposite them turned and met Dvorsky's eyes with a confidence that had only grown with age. "They won't win that fight."

"Can you see what's going to happen?"

"If you mean the fine details of the assault, no. All I'm

certain of is that no one will be able to imprison Artemus and Smokey against their will. Besides, those operatives will have to contend not only with an irate angel and a hellhound, but with six other divine beasts and two of the strongest super soldiers in existence. This battle only has one outcome. Failure." A faint smile curved her lips. "But I believe it will prove useful in...another way."

CHAPTER FIVE

SWEAT DRIPPED DOWN ARTEMUS'S FACE AS HE WORKED the fire between his hands, the gauntlet barely visible beneath the living flames that shrouded it. Wind howled around him, rattling the tarpaulin sheets erected over the gaping holes in the roof and walls of the building.

The biting chill it brought heralded the coming winter.

Though Callie and Sebastian had hired the best construction firm in Chicago to rebuild Artemus's antique shop and Otis's apartment upon their return from Rome, they had decided to hold off until Artemus could approve the architect's plans, something he'd been grateful for when he'd finally emerged from his room a few days ago.

His state of mind until then had been too volatile for him to make any kind of sensible decision.

The look on Drake's face as he'd fallen into Hell was one Artemus had relived during his every waking moment in the two weeks he'd sealed himself off in his room. Though a lot of that time had been spent consoling a broken-hearted Jacob and a devastated Smokey, Artemus had brought up the mental image time and time again, as if to punish himself.

One thing had stood out, always. And it was the one thing Artemus couldn't forgive himself for. Although his twin had been scared and angry, he had also been determined to the very end.

Artemus knew now that Drake had decided to sacrifice himself long before that tragic night in Rome. That he'd understood Artemus would not be able to save him from Samyaza, however much he tried.

Artemus suspected Solomon had known this too. After all, the fallen archangel had come to terms with his own dire fate a long time ago.

But the fact that Drake had asked Artemus to find him before he vanished from this plane of existence could only mean one thing.

He thought he could be saved *after* he'd fallen to Hell.

They both knew their best chance at defeating Satanael and his army of demons lay within their blood bond as Guardian and Key. Because, even though Ba'al had thwarted their attempts to stop Drake from falling to Hell in Rome, the war wasn't over yet.

Light flared as he molded steel, silver, gold, and copper together, the radiance of the rapidly changing molecules casting flickering shadows on the face of the rabbit who sat in a damaged Queen Anne chair to his right.

Smokey huffed as the novel element slowly formed between Artemus's expert hands, his dark eyes reflecting the dazzling sparks as the metals fused into a material unknown to mankind.

Though Artemus could now technically create a weapon anywhere he wished, he still preferred the comfort of the workshop where he'd first learned his metalsmith skills. The old, stone forge lay dark and silent next to the anvil where he finally laid out a glittering, molten sheet.

To his surprise, Sebastian hadn't voiced any questions when Artemus had asked him if he could get his hands on bars of silver and gold. The Englishman had disappeared through a rift and returned two hours later bearing a crate full of the materials Artemus had requested.

"Please tell me you didn't just rob a bank," Daniel had said anxiously while Artemus had examined the glittering contents of the chest.

"Technically speaking, I own that bank," Sebastian had replied evasively.

Artemus spent the next half hour hammering and shaping the alloy into a thin, triangular plate. He submerged it in the slack tub and wiped his brow as it cooled in a giant sizzle of steam.

He turned, took the next bars from the piles stacked neatly beside the forge, and started all over again.

Dusk was falling by the time he finished the twelve plates he'd intended to make that day. Artemus lined them up with the larger ones sitting on the wing-shaped outline he'd drawn out on a table and stepped back, a faint frown on his face.

I'll need at least another twenty smaller plates to complete the structure.

He stretched out the kinks in his neck and winced as he massaged his stiff shoulders. The pain where his missing wing had been had faded to a dull ache. Conrad Greene had healed the wound after he'd changed back to his human form in Rome and all that remained of the injury

Drake had inflicted on him were the faded birthmarks where the appendage had once been.

He was about to call it a day when the pressure inside the workshop shifted in a way he was all too familiar with.

Artemus stiffened. He moved, his hand automatically reaching for the thin, pale blade resting against the stone forge while he whipped out the knife tucked in his boot. Smokey jumped off the chair and swelled into his dark hellhound shape as he bounded over to his side.

The first demons appeared outside the jagged frame that remained of the back door. They ripped through the tarpaulin as if it were paper and came at him with hellish screeches.

The air shimmered around Artemus and Smokey.

The demons smashed against the freshly erected divine barrier around the angel and the hellhound, their ochre eyes flaring with surprise. Their hateful screams grew louder as they glared at the blinding being descending from the second floor of the building.

Otis was in his seraph form, faint lines framing his blazing third eye in a frown and his palms glowing with power as he shielded Artemus and Smokey from attack.

Since the divine barrier Michael and Sebastian had originally raised around the building had yet to be repaired, Otis had insisted on accompanying Artemus whenever he came to Old Town. He'd spent his time salvaging what he could from the smashed-up shop and his apartment while Artemus had worked in the smithy over the past few days.

"I can take them on," Artemus said.

The seraph glanced at him before focusing his attention on the demons multiplying outside the dome. The fiends soon blotted out the darkening sky and the stars popping up in the inky firmament.

Artemus frowned. "Let me do this, Otis."

Guilt flashed on the seraph's normally serene face.

Artemus swallowed a sigh. He knew Otis still blamed himself for what he'd done to him in Rome, just as Sebastian and Daniel continued to do.

Although Artemus had wanted nothing more than to beat them to a pulp at the time they'd physically stopped him from following Drake into Hell, he'd known, even then, that they were doing the right thing. But no amount of words could rid the three men of the burden they bore.

Artemus realized the scars from that battle needed time to heal, for all of them.

A howl rent the air, startling him and the seraph. Smokey had thrown his head back and was baying at the roof, the sound he made full of rage. Otis hesitated before pulling the shield back.

Artemus shifted into his angel form and bared his teeth, his bond with the hellhound a bright band of power connecting their souls.

Both he and Smokey needed this fight.

The switchblade in his right grip lengthened and broadened into a sword swarming with the Flame of God as they charged the demons. Black blood splashed across Artemus's face and Smokey's hide as they carved through the fiends, blades slashing and teeth and claws ripping through the creatures' pestilent bodies.

It didn't take long for Artemus to realize something wasn't quite right.

A thread of disquiet wormed its way through him as the air around him clouded with the fading glow of demon ash.

By the time he sliced the head off the last demon, Artemus was frowning heavily. He stabbed his swords into the ground in front of him and panted slightly as he shifted back to his human form. His ears popped, the room pressure returning to normal. Smokey shook himself out into the Rex rabbit and let out a satisfied huff.

Otis faltered, still in seraph form.

"It's okay." Artemus was unable to mask the bitter bite in his voice. "They're not coming back."

Otis dropped to the ground and changed into his human shape. "This wasn't a true assault."

Unease darkened his eyes as he watched the ash clouds dissipate in the wind.

"No, it wasn't." Artemus clenched his jaw. "They were testing the waters."

Otis stared at him, puzzled.

"They wanted to see what I could do with a single wing."

Otis's eyes widened with alarm.

Artemus fisted his hands. He knew all too well that not being able to fly put him at a disadvantage when it came to fighting Ba'al. Though his preternatural speed and strength had not diminished, he was ten times more powerful in the air than he was on the ground.

And it seemed the enemy was now aware of this damning fact too.

CHAPTER SIX

SERENA OPENED THE GLASS DOOR AND STEPPED INSIDE the bar. She paused on the threshold, the warm air blasting from the overhead heater taking away some of the chill from her bomber jacket and jeans. Though it was close to midnight, the tavern was packed; located a short walk from Grant Park, the place was popular with tourists and locals alike.

Serena scanned the sleek granite counter, the aged wooden floors, and the exposed metalwork making up the ceiling with an experienced eye.

The sound of bullets will definitely be loud in this place. I'm glad I brought the suppressors.

She navigated the pack of people at the bar, ordered a beer, and headed into the games room, her Sigs and blades a comfortable weight under her jacket.

Lou and a man she didn't recognize were playing pool at the far end of the room. Serena noted Tom chatting with a pretty blonde next to a jukebox and a host of familiar and unfamiliar faces dotting the chamber.

Her old team was here, along with what looked and smelled like a group of Immortal operatives.

She swallowed a tired sigh. *Great.*

Lou straightened when he spotted her. "Hey."

His lips curved in a smile that didn't quite reach his pale gray eyes.

"Hey yourself."

Serena stopped beside a metal support bracing the ceiling to the left of the table. She leaned a shoulder against the column and crossed her ankles with a casual air that belied the sudden tension in the room.

Lou carefully put his cue down and studied her with a calculating expression. "Did you think about what I told you earlier?"

Serena had not been too surprised when he had called her a couple of hours ago to tell her he and her former team had been assigned the mission of taking Artemus and Smokey in. Lou counted among the strongest super soldiers in existence today and their associates didn't fall shy of that category either. It was the reason they'd been the most highly sought-after group of mercs in the world this past decade.

Serena knew the offer to capture Artemus and Smokey would have been too lucrative for Gideon Morgan to refuse. She suspected the genius super soldier had wrangled his hands onto some much-coveted defense contracts in the process of negotiating this particular deal.

I'm gonna punch that asshole next time I see him.

In deference to the fact that they were friends, Lou had rung her earlier that night to warn her they'd landed in Chicago. What had come next was a simple demand.

Hand Artemus and Smokey over and no one would get hurt.

Serena masked a frown. *Ivan was right. They're playing real dirty getting the super soldiers involved in this.*

She finally answered Lou's question.

"I did." Serena bared her teeth in the semblance of a smile. "The answer is no. The fuck is implied, obviously."

Lou's expression grew shuttered.

The Immortal opposite him sighed.

Serena observed the man. He was tall and broad-shouldered, with muscles that indicated he worked out every day. If it hadn't been for the intelligent light in his brown gaze, she would have put him down as a steroid junkie.

"Who's your boyfriend?"

Lou grimaced. Someone who sounded suspiciously like Tom snorted behind her.

The Immortal didn't take offence. "I'm Malcolm Greer."

He offered Serena his hand.

She didn't shake it. "You realize the true leaders of the Immortals don't want you involved in this, right?"

Greer's eyes grew flinty in the face of her stare. "We owe a duty to the United Nations and the world. This means there are times when we have to defy those who rule us." He paused. "'Specially when it's clear Artemus Steele and the hellhound are being targeted by Ba'al."

Serena kept her expression neutral. She wasn't surprised the Immortals and the super soldiers already knew of Artemus's encounter with demons that evening.

"Come on, girl." Tom came up and draped an arm around Serena's shoulders, the blonde Immortal trailing behind him. "You know this is the right thing to do. Artemus and the pooch have to be protected. If we'd been utter bastards, we would already have stormed the mansion and captured that loud-mouthed angel and the rabbit by now."

Serena moved.

Tom grunted as he was slammed face-first into the pool table, his arms twisted sharply behind his back. "Ouch!"

"This is gonna be like El Salvador all over again," a female super soldier observed morosely.

"Let him go," Lou said quietly.

Serena met her friend's cold stare. She waited a second longer before releasing Tom. The red marks on the super soldier's skin faded as he straightened and rubbed his wrists.

"What'd you do that for?" Tom asked, sounding genuinely hurt.

Several super soldiers rolled their eyes.

"Let this serve as a warning." Serena looked around the room and met the gazes of her old teammates. "We may have fought alongside each other once. But, in this fight, I *will* take you down if I have to."

The challenge she issued brought a hard light to the eyes observing her.

"You seem inordinately confident in your abilities," Greer said. "We outnumber you by five to one. It would be best if you just surrendered the angel and the hellhound. We don't want to hurt you."

Serena narrowed her eyes slightly at his dismissive tone. If Artemus had been in the room, she suspected Greer would have been a bloody stain on the wall by now.

She arched an eyebrow at Lou. "Do they even know what the divine beasts are capable of?"

An uncomfortable look danced across the super soldier's face.

"Mr. Morgan provided us with a report on the abilities of the Chimera, the Colchian Dragon, the Sphinx, and the Phoenix," Greer said. "They will be difficult adversaries to overcome, I'm sure. Difficult, but not impossible."

"You know there's two more, right?" Serena said, trying not to grind her teeth at the Immortal's condescending words.

"The girl and the boy?" Greer frowned. "They won't be a problem. As for the seraph, I hear he doesn't know how to fight."

Serena didn't know whether to laugh or cry at this.

"Jesus." She sighed and rubbed a hand down her face. "You guys are gonna be roadkill by the time we're done with you."

The super soldiers and the Immortals stiffened at her words.

Lou frowned. "We may struggle to win a fight against the Guardians, but you and Nate are known quantities."

"I doubt that," Serena retorted.

Tom scoffed. "Oh, come on. You're good, but the two of you can't take on all of us."

Serena downed her beer and placed the empty bottle on the edge of the pool table. "Normally, I would agree. But things are different now."

Tom scowled. "Oh yeah? Different how?"

Serena smiled. "Because Nate and I can do this."

She placed a hand against the metal support she'd been leaning against.

Pale light exploded across her skin and spread up the column.

Surprised gasps rose around her as the radiance multiplied, snaking across the beams in the ceiling. Serena held Lou's gaze and flexed her fingers slightly.

Metal screamed and twisted. The ceiling sagged under the distorted joists, raining fine plaster dust around them. Panicked shouts ripped the air as members of the public hastily vacated the games room.

"Don't worry," Serena told Lou and Greer. "It won't come down on you." She tucked her hands in the pockets of her jacket and observed them with a steadfast gaze. "You are not our enemy. But if you come for Artemus and Smokey. If you dare try and rip our family apart, we *will* destroy you."

With that, she twisted on her heels and followed the flow of the crowd out into the street. By the time she made it back to the mansion, Serena was certain the super soldiers and the Immortals wouldn't attack that night. She smiled grimly as she climbed off her bike and removed her visor.

Her little demonstration had served its purpose.

Her smile faded a little as she stared at her hand. Both she and Nate had been shocked by how much stronger they'd become in the last couple of weeks. Every battle with Ba'al seemed to gift them with yet another power, and a strength that seemed to be growing closer and closer to that of the Guardians.

When Serena had first sensed the divine energy within the nanorobots inhabiting her blood and flesh, she'd thought it an accidental coincidence of living in such close quarters with Artemus and the others. Her suspicions had been confirmed when Sebastian had first come to the mansion and explained his theory behind their newly acquired abilities.

But their battle in Rome when Daniel had awakened a few months ago and their more recent fights with Ba'al had made it clear there was more going on than mere serendipity.

Serena recalled what her father had told her a fortnight ago at the Vatican. That her and Nate's path had always been destined to lead them to Artemus and the Guardians. That their destinies were intimately intertwined with those of the ones fated to fight Satanael and his army at the End of Days.

Serena wasn't a religious person. And she knew half the Guardians weren't either. But whoever had gifted them their powers didn't seem to mind this fact. And it made her wonder.

In this world, it was easy for evil to overcome good. She had seen it time and time again with her own eyes, after she'd been rescued from the facility in Greenland. Yet, good kept rising and persevering in the face of cruel adversity and overwhelming odds.

Most would call this foolishness. But Serena's musings told her otherwise.

Like rivers carving valleys out of mountains, like water reshaping an ugly rock into a beautiful pebble, good had a habit of winning in the end.

A noise at the rear of the mansion drew her attention as she headed for the front door. She frowned, retraced her steps, and went round the side of the manor house. Her breath caught when she reached the backyard.

"Goddammit!" Artemus cursed colorfully where he floated fifteen feet in the air.

The angel scowled as the prosthetic appendage he'd painstakingly made broke apart on his back and thudded onto the dirt. He came down unsteadily, his good wing bracing the air at odd angles to stabilize his descent. He still landed on his ass despite this.

"Maybe you should stop for the night," Callie said anxiously where she stood on the back porch, her arms around a wide-eyed Jacob while Smokey yawned at their feet.

Sebastian, Otis, and Nate stood beside her, their expressions tense.

Serena crossed the ground to where Artemus had climbed to his feet and was gathering the pieces of the wing under the watchful eyes of Gertrude. "I thought you said it wasn't going to be ready for another couple of days."

"I know. But it was large enough to at least test." Artemus clenched his jaw. "It looks like I'll have to find another way to make the plates stick together. I thought my divine energy would be enough."

Serena frowned. "Why don't you just fuse them?"

"He cannot," Sebastian said. "The whole requirement of a wing is for its elements to be movable. Hence why he used the most malleable metals in existence to make them."

Otis rubbed his chin thoughtfully. "The only way he's going to be able to fly with a fixed wing is with some kind of jetpack."

Artemus grimaced. "No one's sticking thrusters up my ass." He glowered at the prosthetic wing. "I can make it work. I know I can!"

"Well, you'd better do it fast," Serena muttered.

Nate straightened at her words. The others stiffened.

"They'll come for Artemus and Smokey tomorrow," Serena said grimly in response to their questioning stares. "I'm sure of it."

CHAPTER SEVEN

"ARE YOU SURE IT'S SAFE TO BE HERE?" LEAH MURMURED.

"They're gonna be hard pressed to justify attacking us in broad daylight with so many witnesses around," Serena replied sedately.

Jacob ignored their conversation, his attention focused on the bright lights and colorful stalls around them. He gazed in wide-eyed wonder at the pretty booths and displays, his gloved hand locked tightly around Callie's.

It was Saturday morning and they were at an early Christmas market in Near North Side, just off Chicago's main shopping strip.

Artemus was still in two minds about the plan the super soldier had laid out to them last night. On the one hand, it was a genius idea. On the other hand, a lot of innocent people could get hurt if the super soldiers and Immortal operatives brought the fight to them here and things got ugly.

Elton had not been too pleased about their scheme when he'd called Artemus for an update that morning and neither had Jeremiah when Leah had told him what might go down in the city today.

He frowned faintly. *It might have been better for us to stay at the mansion after all.*

Leah shivered against the cold and tucked her woolen hat over her ears. Haruki edged closer and wrapped an arm around her waist. She sighed as his body heat washed over her. The thick sweater and coat the Dragon wore over his jeans and shirt masked the flames boiling inside his belly.

"He's like her own personal radiator," Artemus muttered in disgust.

"Jealousy is an ugly thing, Artemus," Sebastian said.

"Amen," Daniel murmured.

"Technically speaking, Haruki *is* his wife," Serena pointed out.

Artemus and Haruki scowled at her.

A merry tinkle sounded ahead of them. Smokey's collar was wine red, as was the leather leash it was attached to. The twin silver bells suspended from the lead at the base of his throat contrasted prettily with his rich, chocolate fur as he hopped nimbly through the crowd. This, combined with his butter-wouldn't-melt expression, was drawing enough corny smiles and murmured "oohs" and "aahs" from the people around them to make Artemus want to roll his eyes hard.

"I'm surprised he agreed to wear that," Otis told Artemus. "He normally eats the ones you make for him."

"Callie bribed him with a month's worth of Kobe beef," Artemus muttered irately.

Smokey let out a shameless huff.

"Money talks," Callie said.

"Yeah, well, maybe I should raise your rents," Artemus grumbled.

This earned him a battery of baleful stares.

"Like hell you will," Serena snapped.

Jacob stopped suddenly, his gaze locked on a food stand. A sliver of drool dribbled out the corner of Smokey's jowls as he stared in the same direction. Two minutes later, the young Guardian and the rabbit were face deep in pink candy floss.

"This is nice." Callie hooked an arm through Nate's elbow, her expression relaxed. "It's rare we get to spend time like this."

Despite his misgivings about today's plans, Artemus had to concur. They'd been so busy fighting Ba'al these past few months they'd forgotten what it meant to have fun.

Jacob caught up to him and grabbed his hand.

"Father would have liked this," the boy murmured, his dark eyes solemn.

Surprise jolted Artemus. His chest tightened as he recalled the ones they had recently lost. In another life, he was certain he and Solomon would have been great friends.

"I bet he would." Artemus paused. "You have candy floss on your nose."

Jacob grinned as Artemus wiped the sticky blob away.

"You'll make a good father one day," Callie observed.

"Shut up," Artemus mumbled, his ears warming.

A contented silence fell over their group as they navigated the noisy mass of people filling the plaza and Michigan Avenue.

The peaceful mood didn't last long.

They were negotiating the crowd milling along the River Esplanade when they spotted the first super soldiers on the other side of the road. Lou, Tom, and a group of eight men and women matched their pace as they headed toward DuSable Bridge.

Tom caught their eye and waved at them with a friendly smile. Haruki gave him a cold grin in return and slowly flipped a finger at him above Leah's head. Daniel sighed and begged the Lord for forgiveness.

The super soldier's smile faded to a hard stare.

"Stop antagonizing them," Serena muttered.

"I can't help it," Haruki grumbled in a hurt tone. "I thought we were friends after what happened in Rome."

"We *are* friends." Serena narrowed her eyes at Lou. "We just happen to be on conflicting sides of the same argument right now."

Artemus grimaced. "Well, Plan A failed. Looks like they don't give a damn about witnesses."

Sebastian turned and raised an eyebrow at Serena. "I guess we go with Plan B?"

She nodded before glancing at Leah and Otis. "The middle of the bridge, like we talked about."

The two of them dipped their heads, their faces uneasy.

The DuSable Bridge was four hundred feet long and nearly a hundred feet wide. Once the biggest double-deck bascule bridge in the world, it was still considered one of Chicago's prettiest historic landmarks in this day and age.

Artemus blew out a sigh. *Let's hope it stays that way.*

They hugged the east pedestrian walkway until they got to the wide, serrated, twin metal strips dissecting the center of the bridge. By then, the Immortals and super soldiers converging on them from both ends of Michigan Avenue had made their presence conspicuous.

Artemus stepped into the slow-moving traffic with the

others. They ignored the blast of horns and angry shouts directed at them and took up position near the metal median running along the bridge.

Serena waited until their enemy was on the overpass before barking, "*Now!*"

The sky darkened as Leah shifted into the Nemean Lion amidst them. She snatched the ornate pendant from her neck and raised the spear it transformed into toward the sky, her pupils glowing gold at the same time her hair thickened and her nails sharpened to vicious claws. Electricity sparked the air and ricocheted off the limestone bridge houses at the ends of the overpass. Thunder rumbled. Lightning bloomed overhead.

She brought a bolt of dazzling light down onto the bridge and blew out every electronic device in a one-mile radius of their position with an EMP blast.

Otis morphed into the seraph. His hair brightened to gold. Divine light exploded around his armor-plated body as brilliant white wings flared from his back. He pushed out the barrier he'd projected and forcibly moved the vehicles and bystanders around them off the bridge.

Metal crunched and tires whined as cars, lorries, and motorbikes bumped unceremoniously into one another on both levels of the overpass, drowning out the startled cries of the people who suddenly found their bodies being manipulated onto dry land by an invisible yet gentle power.

Otis thickened his shield a moment later, sealing them off from the outside world and making everything beyond the dome blurry and indistinct.

Protected from curious eyes, Artemus and the rest of the Guardians finally transformed. Otis ascended into the air above them, his third eye and palms bright as he maintained the barrier.

He would try and keep the damage to a minimum while they fought.

Having paused to examine the supernatural wall that had appeared around them with wary gazes, the Immortals and the super soldiers stopped some twenty feet from where Artemus and the others stood in a wide, defensive circle. Surprise widened the eyes of those who were witnessing the angel and the divine beasts' true forms for the first time.

Tom gazed uneasily at the giant, serpentine beast with the halo of snake heads and the sinuous, spiky tail beside the Chimera. "He's big."

"*I'm a she, you fool,*" the Lernaean Hydra hissed.

"Oh God." The Immortal next to Tom paled. "It can talk?!"

The Hydra scowled at the man before glancing at Artemus and Serena. "*Permission to eat our enemy?*"

"Permission denied!" Artemus and Serena snapped.

"You are grounded if you do that," Callie told Jacob firmly.

The Hydra and her host let out a twin, long-suffering sigh. "*Alright then, how about a nibble?*"

Smokey huffed and clawed the ground with a soup-plate-sized paw, his expression similarly enthused.

"Do not even think about it," Sebastian warned the hellhound with a scowl. "We are to stop them, not kill them."

Smokey growled his discontent. The Hydra grumbled under her breath.

"Here they come," Haruki said grimly.

CHAPTER EIGHT

SERENA SWOOPED BENEATH A FIST, ELBOWED A SUPER soldier in the face, and kicked an Immortal in the gut. Her pulse stayed steady, her movements swift and certain as she faced off against her former friends and their new allies.

Grunts and curses sounded around her as Artemus and the Guardians engaged their foe. Though they were outnumbered, they were not in the least bit overpowered.

A figure sailed over Serena's head and smashed onto the blacktop a short distance away. Tom blinked at the hazy sky for a couple of stunned seconds before rolling onto his hands and knees.

He spat out blood and glared at Nate. "Oh, you're gonna pay for that, big guy!"

Nate smiled faintly at the threat.

Serena blocked a blow to her head and stared. It was rare for Nate to mock the enemy during a fight. She studied his smug smirk, glanced at where Artemus was kneeing a super soldier in the groin with a similar expression, and bit back a sigh.

Goldilocks must be rubbing off on him.

Callie's scepter danced in her hands as she swatted at the Immortals and super soldiers trying to surround Artemus, mindful to only inflict superficial wounds upon their bodies. The giant snake sprouting from her tailbone and the ones making up her glittering mane hissed and darted threateningly at their adversaries, earning cautious looks and a wide berth.

Shocked cries erupted farther up the bridge when Leah brought lightning down onto a group of super soldiers and Immortals. One of them sat up slowly where she'd landed hard on her back some dozens of feet away. Static sparked across the super soldier's nanorobot, liquid-armor suit as she shook her head dazedly and climbed to her feet. She lifted a hand to her frazzled locks and inhaled sharply.

A scowl darkened her face. "Shit! I just paid $100 for this haircut!"

Leah grinned. "Oh yeah? Well, sucks to be you."

Her smile vanished the next instant.

An angry roar ripped the air.

Haruki darted in front of Leah, his expression furious. A shower of sparks exploded across his back as the bullets aimed at the Nemean Lion smashed harmlessly into his silver scales.

"Damnit, Greer!" Lou barked. "I said no guns!"

"Hey, *we* don't have superpowers and *they* are not exactly making this easy!" Greer snarled as he jumped and narrowly avoided Jacob's barbed tail.

Haruki twisted on his heels and scowled at the men and women who'd shot at Leah. "You bastards!"

"Mmm, Haru," Leah said anxiously. "I'm okay, really."

Haruki ignored her, his cheeks swelling and his chest

expanding to gargantuan proportions as he took a deep breath.

"Shit!" Tom swore. "*Get out of the way!*"

"Please mind the—" Otis started.

The seraph's warning made the air tremble and echoed painfully in everyone's ears just as a jet of flames erupted from the Dragon's jaws. The fire scorched a molten, red strip in the road, missing the Immortals and super soldiers who leapt out of its reach by a hairbreadth. Their enemy watched in horror as the blazing stream carved a jagged opening in the ornate, metal railing overlooking the river, before raising a sizzling path in the water below.

"—bridge," the seraph finished morosely.

He watched the glowing, distorted metal framing the hole cool down with tinkling noises and sighed, the sound making their eardrums vibrate.

Sebastian frowned at Haruki.

The Dragon shrugged, his expression defensive. "What? You would have done the same if they'd fired their guns at Naomi."

"He's right," Callie said grimly. "They'd be toast if they'd tried that with Nate."

The Immortals and super soldiers surrounding her glanced uneasily at one another. So far, Callie hadn't used her flames or her sonic roar on them.

Artemus observed the damage to the bridge with a grimace. "Chase is gonna be pissed."

"If I were you, I would worry less about Leah's father and focus on the bill the city's gonna give you at the end of this," Serena said.

"What do you mean, *me?* This was your idea!" A blade

scraped across the armor covering his left flank. "Hey, I'm having a conversation here!"

Artemus punched the man who'd tried to skewer him in the face.

"I'm so sorry," Daniel murmured to the group of Immortals and super soldiers trapped in the lassoes of fire dangling from his hands. The divine flames making up the ropes sizzled harmlessly against the clothes and armor of their enemy, trapping them without injuring them. "May God forgive you for your sins."

"If you're sorry, then let us go, you stupid priest!" an Immortal yelled.

Daniel narrowed his eyes slightly where he hovered above the bridge, his enormous Phoenix wings thrumming the air with gentle beats. He rose higher and started swinging the lassoes.

"Hey, what the hell are you doing?!" the Immortal said, alarmed.

A peevish smile twisted Daniel's lips.

The man's gaze shifted to the river. "Oh crap."

"You just had to antagonize the giant bird of fire, didn't you?" a super soldier said sullenly, glaring at the Immortal.

Daniel sent his prisoners flying over the railing and into the river with a petulant grin. The men and women's startled screams ended with abrupt splashes.

The priest's expression turned innocent as he faced Artemus and the others' leaden stares. "What?" He shrugged. "They were being noisy."

Serena tensed when Lou finally appeared in front of her. She snatched her blades from the sheaths on her thighs and studied her oldest friend shrewdly.

It had been years since the two of them had faced off

against one another in the combat ring. This fight was going to be different. She could feel it in her bones.

Lou flashed a cold smile at her, the daggers in his hands glinting and the expression in his gray eyes mirroring her own thoughts. He moved.

Serena leaned back sharply, air whooshing out of her lips in a faint hiss. Sparks erupted on her armor as Lou's knives glanced off her chest with a sound that set her teeth on edge.

She jumped backward into a handstand, kicked him in the jaw as she brought her legs up, and started to somersault into the air. A gasp left her as an iron fist closed around her left ankle, halting her movement in mid-air.

The world blurred as Lou swung her above his head and slammed her down onto the bridge.

Dark spots swarmed Serena's vision, her skull connecting sharply with the blacktop. She ignored the brief numbness that shot down her neck and spine, hooked a foot around Lou's calf, and brought the super soldier to the ground.

Lou grunted when Serena sprang up and straddled him, her thighs immobilizing his lower body. He raised his arms and gritted his teeth as he blocked the rapid punches she rained down on his head and chest, flesh meeting flesh with brutal smacks.

Serena gasped as he bucked violently beneath her.

Lou twisted and pinned her to the ground, using the momentum of his larger weight and frame to overpower her. He grabbed her wrists and locked her arms above her head, his mouth splitting in a triumphant grin.

She scowled, wrapped her legs around his hips, and

headbutted him sharply in the face. Lou's nose broke with a loud crunch. He swore.

"Shit! Will you stop squirming?!"

Serena flashed a savage smile at him where she lay trapped beneath his body, her chest heaving with her breaths.

"Anyone else finding that kind of hot and kinky?" Tom mumbled.

Lou and Serena glared at him.

"You're a sick bastard, you know that?" a super soldier told Tom.

Serena clenched her teeth and finally drew on the alien force dwelling deep beneath her skin. Warmth surged through her, the divine energy she had been gifted filling her veins and suffusing the nanorobots that inhabited her flesh and bones.

Though she knew she could defeat Lou without accessing her new powers, she needed to finish this fight now.

Lou's eyes widened as a golden light exploded across Serena's skin and armor. She snatched her right arm free from his grip and slammed a fist into his solar plexus with lightning-fast speed. Air wheezed out of the super soldier as he rose ten feet in the air, Serena leaping upright beneath him. He landed on the spot she had occupied with a thud and rolled sharply, narrowly missing her attack as she stamped down on where his head would have been.

Serena reached for his throat before he could evade her grasp and lifted him bodily into the air. Lou grabbed her wrist with white-knuckled fists, a scowl distorting his features as he struggled to keep his feet on the ground.

"I'm not gonna lie." Serena frowned. "This is gonna hurt like a bitch."

Lou's eyes flared as she drew her other arm back. He clenched his jaw and steeled himself for the punch.

Serena's fist froze an inch from his left cheek. Her pulse jumped.

The pressure on the bridge had just plummeted.

Her ears popped and her breath plumed in front of her face with her next heartbeat.

Demons!

CHAPTER NINE

TENSION COILED THROUGH ARTEMUS AS HE SCANNED THE area beyond Otis's barrier. Despite the corrupt essence he could sense building close to them, he couldn't see any rifts tearing the air.

Greer scowled. "What the hell is going on?"

"We have company," Lou said grimly.

Serena lowered him to the ground and let him go.

"What kind of company?" the Immortal said uneasily.

"The kind with glowing, yellow eyes that eats people," Artemus replied tersely in Lou's stead.

He removed the thin, sheer blade from the strap on his back, snatched his knife from his armored boot, and unleashed the divine broadsword within.

Lou ignored the pale-faced Immortal staring around the bridge and rubbed his throat. The bruises on his skin were already healing thanks to his nanorobots.

He grimaced at Serena. "I can't believe you broke my nose."

"It's your own damn fault," Serena said while Lou tilted

his head back and adjusted the deformation with a couple of twists. "I told you I'd kick your ass."

"She's not wrong," Tom murmured.

A muscle jumped in Sebastian's jawline. "Where are they?"

A lightning ball crackled in his left hand and the whip of Raguel blazed with Heaven's fire in his right as he drew on his divine powers.

Artemus's fingers clenched on his own weapons. "I don't know."

He felt strangely vulnerable all of a sudden and knew the feeling had everything to do with his missing wing. The air around them throbbed with a heavy malevolence that made his skin itch. Still, no demons appeared.

His gaze finally sought the being floating above them. "Otis?"

A faint frown wrinkled the seraph's brow as he studied their surroundings intently.

"I am not sure," he murmured hesitantly. "This feels different from—"

He froze, his wings stilling. Alarm widened his glowing eyes as he stared at the center of the bridge.

Artemus's heart stuttered. *Shit! The river!*

"Run!" he yelled.

Time slowed. The Guardians moved a fraction of a second ahead of the super soldiers and the Immortals, Artemus's warning resonating across their bond well before his shout echoed across the bridge.

The middle of the overpass exploded upward just as Otis flexed his fingers to extend his shield into a sphere that would protect them from the threat ascending from below.

Debris clouded the air within the barrier in a mush-
rooming cloud, deadly fragments of metal and asphalt
hurtling through the atmosphere before striking the ethereal wall. A giant gap appeared as the bridge collapsed
under the brutal weight of the horde of demons who'd
risen from the rift in the river.

Artemus caught a glimpse of boiling, red waters a
heartbeat before a wave of overwhelming pressure
slammed into him, carrying him into the air. His stomach
lurched as he braced his wing and attempted to slow his
flight, his movements clumsy and his head still ringing
from the noise of the detonation.

Sebastian flashed into view beside him and grabbed his
arm, steadying his flight. A sliver of blood coursed down
the Sphinx's left temple where something had sliced his
skin. Two super soldiers and three Immortals dangled from
the triple-thronged whip in his other hand.

Blood thundered in Artemus's veins as the world spun
upright once more. He sheathed his swords, grabbed two
injured Immortals, and carried them to what remained of
the north end of the bridge, Sebastian assisting him.

Their charges landed awkwardly on the cracked blacktop, their expressions dazed as they stared at the fiends
swarming the jagged chasm that now occupied the center
of the overpass.

"Bloody hell," one of the Immortals murmured. "You
guys have been fighting those monsters all this time?!"

Artemus clenched his jaw. *Hell doesn't even begin to
describe it.*

Faint screeches reached his ears. He looked up and saw
the blurred shapes of hundreds of demons battering at the
shield that now encircled them. Otis's barrier was complete

and wouldn't let any more of Hell's forces inside his protective orb.

Artemus scowled. *Still, plenty got through.*

"Stand back." He reached for his blades and moved in front of the stunned Immortals. "You're no match for them."

Sebastian moved into position beside him. Serena, Nate, and Callie appeared on Artemus's other side. Lou joined them, the super soldiers on their side of the divide taking up rear guard.

Beyond the demonic horde and the fissure that had cleaved through the overpass, Haruki, Leah, Smokey, Jacob, and Daniel had formed a wall in front of the injured Immortals on the south half of the bridge. Tom hobbled toward them, left leg bleeding before his nanorobots repaired the injury, the rest of Serena and Nate's old team closing in behind him.

"You should have come with us." Lou looked over at Artemus, a muscle jumping in his cheek. "We could have avoided all of this!"

Artemus met the super soldier's glare with a steady gaze. "Do you really believe you could stop Hell's forces if they wanted to get their hands on me and Smokey?"

Lou did not reply.

"Well, we knew they would come for you," Sebastian murmured. "Still, this is quite the declaration of war."

Serena narrowed her eyes. "Why aren't they attacking?"

A fresh bout of unease darted through Artemus, his thoughts echoing the super soldier's concerns. "I don't know."

He clenched his jaw. *Something isn't right.*

He startled as Otis's voice rumbled across the divine

dome, the power of his words throbbing against his skin and armor.

"Reveal yourself!" the seraph commanded sharply.

Artemus's heartbeat quickened. He had never heard the Voice of God sound so irritated before. He followed the seraph's unblinking gaze to a spot in the midst of the pack of dark-bodied, ochre-eyed fiends.

Fear twisted through him for the first time since he'd lost Drake to Hell. Whatever this was, it was more than just a declaration of war.

His worst misgivings were given life when three figures rose from the horde atop giant, demonic beasts, faces wreathed with contemptuous smiles.

Sebastian swore colorfully.

"Holy shit," Lou mumbled.

"Oh God," Callie whispered numbly.

Ice filled Artemus's veins as he stared at the wicked apparitions.

He couldn't believe they'd been hiding among the army of fiends that had materialized from the rift. And he didn't need Otis to tell him that the three demons who faced them were commanders and Princes of Hell.

Their midnight-black wings, serrated broadswords, oppressive auras, and the monstrous creatures they rode were more than enough to signal their status in Hell's hierarchy. Like Astarte and Beelzebub, these demons' pupils also glowed crimson rather than ochre, indicating their formidable powers.

The pressure wave that knocked us down was from them!

Artemus inhaled shakily. He made a face the next instant.

Lou gagged slightly. "Jesus, they stink."

Callie wrinkled her nose.

The demon commanders smelled worse than a decomposing corpse that had been stuck in a septic tank for a month.

"Maggot. Oriens. Ariton." Otis's voice drew winces and grimaces from the lesser fiends and sent Artemus's pulse into the stratosphere. "You are far from your prison, my fallen brethren."

Callie cast a nervous glance at Sebastian. "Bar the big guys and the ones we've killed, those three form the rest of Hell's Council, right?"

Sebastian dipped his chin, his eyes alight with power and a heavy frown wrinkling his brow. "Yes. Only the four major princes, Samyaza, and Beelzebub are missing. Ba'al did not just bring their cavalry. They brought half their goddamned army."

Artemus's blood pounded heavily in his skull as that unfortunate truth sank in. "Anybody got a Plan C? 'Cause I gotta tell you, I have a very bad feeling about this. The kind of bad feeling that sees me and Smokey ending up in Hell."

Serena's grip tightened on her daggers. "Even if we had a Plan C, I'm afraid these assholes would tear right through it."

The demon commanders' attention remained focused on Otis, as if they judged him to be the most dangerous foe among them.

The one with the squid tentacles sprouting from his body, who sat astride a saber-toothed tiger, finally hissed out a welcome. "And you are far from *His* protection, seraph."

"The Voice of God has lost his touch." The demon

bearing a golden crown and perched on the back of a vicious-looking, mammoth-like creature with bloodied tusks chuckled gleefully. "I can't believe he didn't see us coming. We have nothing to fear from him after all!"

"Come now, brothers." The demon prince with the pulsing, red crown straddling a black dragon that closely resembled the beast Astarte had once ridden observed Otis steadily. "He has been on Earth for too long." His tone turned dismissive. "Besides, he is not yet in full possession of his powers."

"What does he mean by that?" Serena said, startled. "Otis still isn't at full power?!"

Artemus scowled, more irritated at the demon princes for ignoring Otis than shocked by their puzzling words. "No. If I'm not mistaken, there are two more symbols that have yet to manifest on his palm."

These bastards!

He stiffened when Ariton's crimson gaze landed on him.

"Son of Michael and Theia, you shall come with us," the demon prince ordered in a tone that would not brook defiance.

Artemus's knuckles whitened on his swords. Fury surged through him, superseding his fear in a hot flood that made his blood boil. "Like hell I shall!"

Maggot's sibilant voice echoed angrily across the bridge. "Do as you're told, you insolent child!"

"Or what?" Artemus growled. "You're gonna spank me?"

"Er, Artemus?" Callie murmured glassily. "Maybe you should cut back on the trash talk."

Oriens laughed, the sound as cold as ice. "Satanael will

flay you alive when he gets his hands on you, Guardian or not. And I shall eat the bits of flesh that fall off your body!"

Artemus's mouth stretched in a vicious smile. He flipped the finger at the demon princes. "Oh yeah? Well, tell Satan he can kiss my shiny, pink butt, assholes!"

"Wow," Lou mumbled.

"Like a red flag to a bull," Sebastian said glumly.

"*Can you please stop antagonizing the enemy?!*" Serena hissed at Artemus.

"The enemy are douchebags," Artemus retorted.

"Well, I think you just pissed off the douchebags," Callie said grimly, divine flames exploding on her curved horns as she brought forth all of her powers.

"Here they come!" Nate warned.

CHAPTER TEN

SOMETHING THAT FELT LIKE A SLEDGEHAMMER SLAMMED into Serena's midriff. She gasped, air locking in her throat as she skidded backward some dozen feet, the sounds of a furious battle filling her ears.

Damn! They're fast!

A large shape loomed out of the corner of her eye. She twisted and warded off the next strike with her forearms. The impact jarred her bones and made her grit her teeth. She sucked in a breath.

A giant, barbed tail was wedged against her combat suit, the inky spikes scraping against her divine-energy-infused nanorobots. It was taking all of her strength to block it.

Ariton observed her coldly from where he sat astride the dragon that had attacked her. "Interesting."

The demon prince's crimson gaze lingered on the pale light enveloping her liquid-armor suit and shielding her skin. He glanced at Nate where the super soldier fought

Maggot's saber-toothed hellbeast alongside several super soldiers, his body similarly protected by divine radiance.

Ariton dropped down from his dragon, his broadsword brimming with hellfire and the ground trembling briefly under his forceful landing. "You are not creatures of Heaven, yet it seems you have earned the right to possess His powers."

The hairs on Serena's nape rose at the icy rage that flared in the demon prince's eyes when he stepped toward her.

"*That is unforgivable!*" the fallen angel roared, raising his sword.

Serena moved, knowing even as she jumped that she was too slow to evade the blade. Sparks exploded as Ariton's sword clashed against a golden scepter inches from her heart.

"Hey, asshole, how about you pick on someone your own size?!" Callie hissed.

She took a deep breath and released a sonic roar right in Ariton's face, her snakes spitting with fury. Ariton cursed as the attack drove him back a few steps. Serena and Callie danced out of the way of the angry dragon's massive tail.

"I thought we weren't doing bitch talk!" Serena shouted.

"Yeah, well, I changed my mind!"

Callie looked at Sebastian and Artemus as they engaged Maggot, unease darkening her jade eyes.

Serena followed her anxious gaze south to where Daniel, Smokey, and Jacob faced off against Oriens and his monstrous ride on the other side of the chasm cleaving the bridge in two.

It was becoming clear the demon princes were

diverting their attention so as to split up their defenses. Serena frowned.

They're probably hoping the distraction will help them snatch Artemus and Smokey.

The air shimmered with a wave of heat as Ariton's dragon reared back on his hind legs and breathed out a river of fire. The stream of divine flames Callie released from her jaws clashed into the crimson jet with a sound like thunder, halting its deadly progress midway to the group of Immortals and super soldiers the dragon had intended to scorch.

Ariton swung his sword at Serena while the divine beast and the helldragon circled one another. Surprise flashed in his scarlet eyes when she blocked his attack with her crossed blades. Her heels dug into the blacktop, the asphalt cracking as it gave beneath her weight.

Power pulsed through Serena. Her muscles bunched. "Fool me once, shame on you."

Rage distorted the demon prince's nightmarish features as she forced him back a step.

"Fool me twice, shame on me!" Serena snarled.

She dropped, rose beneath her attacker's guard, and punched him in the jaw. Shockwaves rippled through her flesh and bones. Ariton stumbled into the dragon's flank.

"Attagirl!" Lou shouted gleefully from her left. "Oh shit!"

He disappeared under two demons. Greer dived into the melee.

Corruption thickened the air as Ariton straightened to his full height.

"I see the friends of Samyaza's blood are as tiresome as he is," the demon spat.

Serena's heart stuttered. This was the first news of Drake they'd received since he'd fallen to Hell. Rage filled her to the core.

"What have you bastards done to him?!" she growled.

A mocking smile twisted Ariton's mouth. "Don't worry. He's a wily one, but we will soon have our hands on him. He cannot escape Hell through a portal, after all."

Serena's lips parted in surprise. *Wait. Drake isn't their prisoner! But—how?!*

ARTEMUS WIPED BLOOD FROM HIS MOUTH AND PANTED slightly, his heart thumping hard against his ribs. A muffled curse left him as he ducked out of the way of Maggot's sword. The blade carved a sliver of ash-blond hair from his head as it sang past his skull.

"Hey, douchebag! I thought you wanted me alive!" he snarled at the demon prince.

Maggot grinned, all ugly teeth and no humor. "Just like Ramiel, Satan can bring the dead back to life. It's no skin off my nose if I make him indulge in some necromancy."

Sebastian climbed to his feet where the demon prince had knocked him aside.

"You are seriously starting to get on my nerves!" he hissed.

His eyes and palms flashed a vivid white as he harnessed his powers.

Maggot folded his wings around his deformed body as a volley of blazing lighting balls crashed into him. Artemus made the most of the diversion and swung his swords at the demon. The blades carved into Maggot's pinions, drawing black blood.

The demon prince screeched in outrage. "*How dare you!*"

Artemus gasped, Maggot's spiked boot connecting with his gut and denting his armor. He shot backward and collided with Sebastian. They landed on the bridge in a tangle of limbs and wings.

A terrifying roar sounded above them.

Artemus sucked in air, grabbed Sebastian, and rolled them out of the way of the massive paw descending upon them. The helltiger's eyes burned with wrath as he smashed down on the space they had occupied a heartbeat ago.

Artemus glanced at Nate's unconscious form as he and Sebastian climbed to their feet. Relief surged through him.

The super soldier was still breathing despite being brought down by the beast. He stirred and sat up dazedly just as Serena reached his side.

The helltiger howled as a sonic roar blasted into him. His claws carved grooves in metal and asphalt, the force driving into his flank shoving him against the bridge railing. The barrier groaned before giving way beneath his immense weight. He dropped toward the river amidst the broken pieces, all snarls and waving paws.

"Hands off my property, you damn cat!" Callie growled.

Dark blood soaked her skin and writhing mane. She leaned on her scepter, chest heaving.

Ariton's helldragon moaned feebly behind her. The beast lay on his side, an inky pool forming beneath his giant frame where she'd stabbed him in the chest.

Maggot stared at the crimson-tinged waters and

seething rift where his helltiger had disappeared. His enraged shriek echoed in Artemus's ears.

"*You shall pay for that, wench!*"

Sebastian and Artemus moved to intercept the demon prince as he charged Callie. Maggot rocked to an abrupt halt. He straightened, elation filling his crimson eyes.

He turned to stare at the river. "He is here."

Dread churned Artemus's gut at his jubilant tone.

Ariton and Oriens had stopped fighting and were looking in the same direction as Maggot, their expressions smug. The demons who'd engaged the other Guardians and super soldiers stepped back, fear widening their sulfurous pupils.

CHAPTER ELEVEN

EVIL SATURATED THE AIR IN A SUDDEN, THICK SURGE, SO heavy and hateful it caused most of the Immortals and several super soldiers to fall to their knees and clutch at their throats, the corruption robbing them of their breath.

"What is that?" Serena murmured as she joined Artemus, Sebastian, Callie, and Nate behind her.

Artemus followed their frozen gazes to the eastern branch of the Chicago River.

The wave sweeping toward them from the direction of Lake Michigan was visible even through Otis's barrier. The swell accelerated and rose as he watched, the leading edge funneling into a prow.

Artemus's stomach dropped. *That's not natural!*

A colossal shape appeared beneath the turbulent surface. Wicked horns as thick as a bus pierced the foaming breakers.

"Sweet mother of God," Lou mumbled.

Artemus stared, his pulse pounding in his veins.

The creature rising from the river's depths was from man's worst nightmares.

"Is that—?" Callie started, aghast.

"Leviathan," Sebastian growled, his knuckles blanching around Raguel's whip.

Water cascaded down the demonic sea serpent's dark, oily hide as he loomed out of the channel, the torrents crashing into the river and causing it to surge up the embankments.

Leviathan was some three hundred feet tall, with a tail as long as his body and six heads surrounding his primary, horned skull. His crimson gazes were matched by the hundreds of smaller eyes dotting his enormous, leathery wings.

"I think I'm gonna be sick," Greer said hoarsely.

"You and me both, pal," Lou concurred, his face pale.

Artemus's heart thundered in his chest as he gazed upon one of Hell's principal princes. Leviathan's eyes blazed scarlet when they locked onto him and Smokey with unerring precision. Artemus glanced past the gigantic beast.

Shit! Is there another rift in Lake Michigan?!

Panicked shouts echoed from the two halves of the bridge as the serpent twisted his giant tail in a blisteringly fast move that should have been impossible for a beast his size. He smashed down on the shimmering divine shield that lay between him and his targets, his furious roar booming in Artemus's ears.

The barrier trembled but held.

Trees bowed and windows exploded along the facade of the buildings lining the river under the backlash of the violent strike. Terrified screams rose dimly from the crowds who'd stayed back to gawk at the blurry sphere that had enclosed the bridge, the mythical creature now towering over it.

Power throbbed along the bond that linked Artemus to the other Guardians, hot and sudden. They exchanged startled glances before staring at Otis where he hovered above them, wings barely flickering while he stared down the demon prince who had challenged him.

The holy energy was coming from the seraph.

Light flared in his third eye and on his hands, so brilliant it was blinding.

Artemus blinked black spots from his vision and glimpsed a dim shape materializing on Otis's left palm. The third point of his second star wavered and pulsed, ethereal and not quite there.

A memory blasted through Artemus's mind then. One that was not his own.

In that fleeting instant, Artemus saw the seraph's final form through Theia's eyes, as he had appeared during the holy war that had cast Satanael and his followers to the depths of Hell.

Shock had his grip loosening on his blades.

"Artemus?" Sebastian frowned. "What is it?"

"He can fight," Artemus mumbled.

"What?" Callie said. "What do you mean?"

"Otis." Artemus swallowed hard. "He can—"

Leviathan's shriek drowned out the rest of his words. Fire bloomed from the monster's jaws and struck the outer surface of the divine shield. The flames gathered in a focused jet that centered on a point opposite Otis, as if the Prince of Hell wished to incinerate the seraph.

A small fracture appeared in the barrier.

"That's not good," Serena said dully.

Instinct had Artemus searching for Smokey with his gaze.

The three-headed hellhound was staring in his direction from the south half of the bridge. The crack in the divine shield widened.

Artemus frowned at it before looking at Smokey. *Can you hear me?*

The hellhound's reply came immediately. *Yes.*

We must lend him our powers.

I know.

Relief flashed through him. Smokey must have sensed the same thing he'd perceived in the last few seconds. Artemus took a deep breath, raised a hand in the direction of the seraph, and clenched his jaw.

He had once channeled his divine energy into his brother to save him from the demon inside his soul. And he had lent his strength in the same way to Jacob, when the Guardian had been united with his key and begun awakening in the presence of his gate. Everything inside Artemus was telling him he could do the same with Otis across their bond. He focused, flexed his fingers slightly, and poured all of his and Smokey's holy powers into the seraph.

This had better work!

"What are you doing?!" Callie gasped.

Sebastian swore as Artemus and Smokey shrank into their non-divine forms, their bodies unable to keep up their ultimate manifestations while they were temporarily drained of their unearthly strength.

The Guardians must have sensed what was happening across the ties that bound them.

Otis twitched where he floated in the air. His glowing eyes found Artemus. The third inverted V on his left palm solidified.

"Thank you," the seraph murmured, his voice reverberating through Artemus's very soul.

A golden rift tore open next to Otis. He reached inside and withdrew an enormous, golden broadsword awash with Heaven's fire.

"*No!*" Oriens spat. "That's impossible!"

Ariton and Maggot glowered and cursed at the seraph.

Artemus understood then why the demon princes had focused on Otis when they'd first appeared. The seraph's full powers were likely second only to God's.

The barrier dissipated as Otis dropped his shield.

The world held its breath.

Leviathan reared back, his cheeks swelling and a red glow bubbling up his body and his long neck as he prepared to unleash Hell's fire upon his archenemy.

Otis raised his blade. "*You shall not touch them!*"

The seraph's roar caused the clouds to part above the city and made buildings tremble. Glittering fragments filled the air as every window and glass object within a two-mile radius of the bridge disintegrated into a fine powder. Cracks tore along the embankments and down the length of Michigan Avenue, as well as the adjoining roads. The water in the river and the lake receded slightly.

The Immortals and super soldiers who weren't already on their knees fell to the ground, agony twisting their faces as they raised their hands to their bleeding ears. The people still standing in the vicinity of the bridge were unconscious on the ground, their minds unable to bear the divine pressure weighing down on them.

Only the Guardians and Serena and Nate stood untouched by the devastating impact of the seraph's voice.

Leviathan crashed into the next bridge east of their position, the sea serpent driven back some thousand feet by the sheer physical power of the seraph's words. The beast screamed as cuts appeared on his flanks and wings.

Artemus blinked. Now that he wasn't in his angel form, it was difficult for him to follow Otis's movements. All he could see were the wounds being inflicted by an invisible force at a speed that defied reason.

Maggot, Oriens, and Ariton rose to defend their superior, their battle cries rending the air as they flew to Leviathan's aid. They smashed into the river before they could land a single strike on their enemy.

Hellish shrieks exploded as the demons' rift started to shrink.

Artemus knew it wasn't Hell that was doing the closing.

The fiends sprang from the bridge and dove into the swirling, crimson vortex churning the river. They were followed by the hellbeasts, the monsters hauling their injured bodies over the railing and accompanying their masters into the dwindling abyss.

Leviathan was the last one to leave, the sea serpent fighting the current dragging him down to the place where he had been imprisoned for millennia with all his might. His giant, angry eye was the last thing Artemus saw before the portal closed with a sound that put the angel's teeth on edge. A faint, crimson light flared above Lake Michigan as Otis closed the rift the monster had arrived through.

The silence that fell upon the city in the moment that followed was deafening in its suddenness.

"That went well," Sebastian said leadenly.

Artemus's gaze found the seraph coming toward them. By the time he landed on the bridge, Otis had resumed his human appearance and his broadsword had vanished, gone to wherever the holy weapon had been waiting for its rightful owner to claim it.

Artemus took a shaky breath, divine energy filling his soul once more. He looked at Otis's left hand. The symbol that had unlocked the seraph's new powers was no more.

"How the hell did you do that?" Serena murmured, still shocked.

"I—I don't know," Otis replied awkwardly.

He didn't meet Artemus's eyes. Artemus bit back a sigh. He could tell his assistant was lying.

"That was *amazing!*"

Jacob's excited voice grew closer as Daniel carried him and the rest of the Guardians across the gaping chasm that separated them.

"Yeah, dude." Admiration sparkled in Haruki's eyes. He landed on the blacktop and came toward them with the others. "Color me impressed."

Otis flushed under their wondering gazes.

Smokey darted over and bumped his head against Artemus's right ankle.

"Hey, pooch." Artemus picked him up and gazed into his bright, chocolate eyes, relief dancing through him. Hell hadn't managed to claim either of them today. "You did well."

Smokey huffed and bit his nose.

Artemus swore, yanked the rabbit off his face, and held him at arm's length. "Why, you little—!"

"*Leah!*"

Artemus turned. Jeremiah had jumped out of a police

car at the north end of the bridge and was jogging toward them, deftly avoiding the uneven, cracked blacktop and the debris littering the ground as he aimed for his daughter.

The sounds of sirens finally registered on Artemus's radar. He looked along the length of Michigan Avenue and spotted the multitude of patrol cars and ambulances bearing down on them.

"How about you rift us out of here?" he muttered to Sebastian.

"I am afraid my powers are a bit too depleted for that right now."

Jeremiah hugged Leah tightly, his eyes flashing with a murderous light as he narrowed them at Artemus over her shoulder.

"Great," Artemus said morosely. "Just great."

Daniel was staring at the buildings along the river. "Did we break the city?"

Callie sighed. "Yeah."

Jacob beamed, as if this news was a source of immense pride. Without Solomon's calming influence, Artemus suspected the kid would grow into a bloodthirsty warrior, courtesy of the cantankerous beast who inhabited his soul.

"There's something I need to tell you," Serena said.

Artemus frowned. Though she had addressed them all, her eyes were focused on him and Smokey.

"Ariton mentioned something during our fight." Serena took a shallow breath, a muscle dancing in her cheek. "He said they hadn't gotten their hands on Drake yet."

"What?" Callie mumbled in the shocked silence.

Serena made a face and raked her hair with a hand. "It seems Drake has been hiding in Hell all this time, some-where out of their reach. And it sounds as if the demons are controlling all portals out of the Underworld so he can't escape through one of them."

Artemus's legs went weak. Relief, affection, and regret twisted through his soul in equal measure, while a hundred thoughts raced through his mind. He looked at Smokey, a single one dominating them all. The rabbit growled, his eyes flashing crimson.

Artemus swallowed. *Drake hasn't given up!*

The idea that had formed briefly in his mind during the battle that had just rocked Chicago came to him once more. A shout distracted him before he could put voice to it. He twisted on his heels.

Elton was headed toward them, his face like thunder.

"Seriously, rift us out of here," Artemus begged Sebastian.

CHAPTER TWELVE

ARTEMUS WALKED INTO THE KITCHEN AND ROCKED TO A halt. He scowled at Lou. "What the hell are you doing here?"

"And good morning to you too, Mr. Grumpy." Lou finished making his coffee before joining Serena where she sat cleaning her guns at the table. "Is he always this pleasant in the morning?"

"Sometimes he bites," Serena muttered.

"You'd better not have moved in while I was sleeping," Artemus threatened.

He marched over to the refrigerator, grabbed a carton of orange juice, and poured himself a glass. He hesitated before grabbing some painkillers from a drawer.

The headache pounding his temples had as much to do with the three-hour-long tirade he'd had to suffer at the hands of Elton and Jeremiah upon their return to the mansion as it did with yesterday's clash with Ba'al.

That no fatalities had been recorded among the public was a miracle all of them were eternally thankful for. Bar a few broken limbs, the Immortals and the super soldiers tasked with taking Artemus and Smokey into custody had also escaped their encounter with the demons with only minor injuries.

Artemus wondered whether Otis had had something to do with their extraordinary luck. He suspected the seraph wouldn't admit to it even if he asked.

The Vatican organization and the U.N. Special Security Council had taken charge of handling the city's officials and the press in the aftermath of the epic battle that had damaged half the Loop and a considerable area of the Near North Side, something Artemus was begrudgingly grateful for. He didn't want to owe anything to the people who'd attempted to imprison him and Smokey.

He grimaced as he downed his tablets. *I don't even want to know what kind of cockamamie story they cooked up to explain what happened yesterday.*

"Hell has come to Earth," Haruki said in a grave voice.

Artemus stiffened and turned to stare at the Yakuza heir.

Haruki sat cross-legged on the window seat, his computer on his lap and Smokey snoozing beside him. After much pleading from Jeremiah, Leah had stayed the night at her father's, more for the detective's nerves than her own.

"What?"

"I'm just quoting the Tribune's front-page headline," Haruki explained at the sight of Artemus's wary expression. "All the news outlets are pretty much reporting the same thing." He looked at Serena. "Blowing out the city's cameras and electronic devices with an EMP pulse was a genius idea. There are no recordings of what happened, just witness accounts, so our identities are safe."

"Yeah, well, this isn't my first rodeo," Serena murmured.

Nate and Callie sauntered into the kitchen, Callie clinging to the super soldier's arm.

"I'm sorry," Nate said. "I'll start on breakfast."

"You know there's nothing in your lease that says you have to cook every day, right?" Artemus muttered.

"I know. But I like it."

A loud rumble echoed across the kitchen. Smokey opened an eyelid and yawned before licking his chops hungrily.

Nate smiled faintly. "I'll make some bacon first."

"I'd start by hiding the hickeys on your neck before the others see them, if I were you," Lou said mildly.

Callie didn't even blush. Nate raised a hand to the fresh bruises on his skin, ears turning beetroot red.

"I'll go grab a sweater," the super soldier murmured before disappearing hastily.

"It's like she's marking her territory," Artemus said in a disgusted voice to no one in particular.

Callie grinned.

"Haruki, go kiss your husband," Serena ordered. "He needs attention."

The Dragon flipped her the finger.

Artemus turned to Lou. "And you," he said warily. "What did you mean, the 'others'?"

"The mansion didn't have enough rooms, so most of us camped outside," Lou replied with a nonchalant shrug.

Suspicion brought a scowl to Artemus's brow. A threatening squawk rose from the backyard. He strode to a window and yanked the curtains aside.

Tents rose amidst the gravestones dotting the rear garden. Tom stood outside one of them. He was facing off against Gertrude while Henrietta and Charlene watched diligently from the sidelines.

Artemus glared at Serena and Lou over his shoulder. "The hell?!"

"I distinctly told you they were gonna stay the night," Serena said without a trace of remorse.

She holstered her guns and took a sip of her coffee.

"Oh yeah? Was that before or while Elton and Jeremiah were yelling at me?" Artemus waved a hand irritably. "And don't you guys have—safehouses or something?"

"We do." Lou grinned. "But it's more fun here."

Artemus glowered at the super soldier.

Nate returned. Sebastian trailed behind him, feet bare and hair in disarray.

The Englishman had become more relaxed in the past few weeks. Artemus suspected this had as much to do with him lowering the rigid defenses he had maintained for so long as it did with the woman he was now dating.

Lou studied the Englishman's flamboyant peignoir with a leaden expression.

"It grows on you," Serena told Lou.

Alarmed shouts reached them from the yard.

"What is that infernal noise?" Sebastian muttered.

"The chicken is chasing Tom," Artemus said contemptuously. "And the goat is chewing on a tent."

Nate sighed and went to open the back door. "Gertrude, stop harassing the nice super soldier." He paused. "There's a good hen. Daisy, synthetics are bad for your digestion, so no more eating tents, please. I'll bring you some fresh hay after breakfast."

"Shoot me," Artemus said glumly. He frowned faintly at Sebastian. "Where's Otis?"

Artemus's assistant was rooming down the hall from Sebastian. Though he'd insisted he wanted to return to his apartment above the antique shop once the building work was complete, Artemus secretly hoped he would stay permanently.

"Still recharging his batteries. I suspect he will sleep the whole day."

They were halfway through breakfast when Elton, Leah, and Jeremiah showed up.

"Hey." Leah walked over to Haruki and leaned down to kiss him. She froze when she saw her father's expression and dropped a chaste peck on the Yakuza heir's cheek instead. "How was your night?"

"Noisy." Haruki narrowed his eyes at Callie. "Callie didn't let Nate sleep until the morning."

Jeremiah's scowl threatened to take over his entire face.

Callie bit into her eggs with an innocent smile.

Artemus eyed the vein throbbing in Elton's temple and decided to wait until he'd eaten something before questioning him.

"So, how are things with the city?"

Elton ripped a chunk from a loaf of fresh bread and buttered it with controlled violence. "How do you think they are?"

Artemus made a face. "That bad, huh?"

"Things could have been much worse," Lou said mildly. "At least Leviathan didn't get his hands on Artemus and the pooch."

Elton and Jeremiah paled at that.

A sound came from the direction of the foyer. Jacob

shuffled into view in his pajamas, feet dragging. He blinked sleepily, looked around the table, and crawled onto Serena's lap.

The super soldier stiffened. She faltered before closing her arms awkwardly around the snoozing child. Jacob snuggled into her chest and closed his eyes.

Callie grinned. Leah smiled.

"Don't let Tom see you like that," Lou told Serena. "His ovaries might explode."

Serena rolled her eyes at him before looking at Artemus. "So, what now?"

Artemus put down his fork and knife. "Can I take a look at your liquid-armor disc?"

A puzzled frown wrinkled Serena's brow. "Sure."

She reached inside the pocket of her cargo pants and handed over the metal device that contained the nanorobot combat suit.

Artemus examined the hardware closely before looking at the super soldiers. "Take me to Gideon."

They blinked in surprise.

"What do you want with Gideon?" Lou asked guardedly.

"I got an idea yesterday. About my wing."

Artemus narrowed his eyes at the disc in his hand. *I need to get to Drake before Satanael and Samyaza find him.*

CHAPTER THIRTEEN

Drake masked his distaste as he eyed the small, roasted reptile on the end of his knife.

Astarte let out a low grunt. "Stop playing with your food and eat it, kid."

She skewered the darkening flesh of the two creatures sizzling above the fire pit with her spear and crunched them down in a couple of bites, bones and all. She licked her lips before nodding her thanks to the demon who'd brought them the serving of freshly killed helllizards.

Drake ignored the lower fiend's nervous ochre glance, sighed, and bit into the reptile. It was his first meal in two days and he couldn't afford to be picky.

To his surprise, the helllizard didn't taste as disgusting as he had feared. It was miles better than the eel-like creature Astarte had given him the first week he landed in Hell but not as nice as the hellboar they'd had a few days back.

The Underworld wasn't at all what Drake had expected it to be. Instead of eternal fire and damnation, the place was a never-ending maze of gloomy caves, dark forests, and tunnels, interspersed with lakes and seas in which night-marish shapes lurked. Some of the caverns he and Astarte had traversed in the last two weeks had been large enough to house cities and mountains and were often crowned with clouds of sulfur and mist. At times, Drake thought he'd glimpsed the crimson fires of demonic settlements in the far distance.

Astarte had steered well clear of them. When he'd asked her why, her reply had been curt. "They are faithful to Satanael."

"So, we're staying here for a while?" Drake said once he'd swallowed his last bite of helllizard.

He glanced around the cave they were presently hiding in and at the horde of demons hovering outside. The fiends were Astarte's faithful followers and had shown him no hostility since he first met them a week ago. The fact that they could sense Samyaza's blood inside his veins might have had something to do with their uneasy deference.

"Yes. We leave in the morning."

Drake didn't comment on the fact that it was kinda hard to tell when it was morning or night in Hell. There was no sky down here and what could have passed for stars were actually millions of glow worms covering the ceilings and walls of the caverns. He suspected the demons had developed some kind of internal clock over time that kept them attuned to the world above them.

At least my watch still works. He glanced at his left wrist with a faint frown. *Which is kinda weird too.*

"Where are we going?" he asked Astarte.

The demon goddess's eyes gleamed as she studied him across the fire pit. "We head into Hell Deep, where one of our allies is. Now sleep, son of Samyaza. I shall keep first watch."

She indicated the pallet in a corner of the cave, grabbed her spear, and made for the exit.

Drake grimaced but didn't say anything as he headed over to the makeshift bed made from wood and the skins of dead monsters. He owed the former Babylonian goddess his life, after all.

The details of what had happened after he had let go of Artemus and been dragged into Hell by Belial were still etched starkly in his mind. As he'd fallen through the inter-dimensional portal Ba'al's leader had opened up to claim him, the corrupt forces storming the crimson rift had made Samyaza's life force surge through his soul with a vengeance. Two things had stopped him from losing himself to the darkness inside him.

The first had been his goddess mother's protective bonds. Though her reach was thin and intangible within Hell's domain, Theia's powers had nonetheless wrapped around the core of who he was and protected his mind and heart from surrendering to his father's evil.

The second and most shocking had been his shield.

The weapon had briefly expanded into a sphere that had broken Belial's grip on Drake as they descended into Hell and cast him along a different path through the Underworld. The next thing he'd known, he'd been plunging inside a foggy canyon in his human form, Belial's scream of fury fading in his ears as he spun helplessly in sulfur-tainted air.

It was Astarte who had saved him that day.

As he'd glimpsed the rapidly approaching ground and the forest he was headed for with growing panic, inky wings had opened up beneath him and a figure had darted up in his direction from a clearing. Fear had overcome alarm briefly when Drake had seen the face of the demon goddess rising toward him. But instead of slashing his powerless form into pieces with her viper-wreathed spear, Astarte had caught him before he smashed into the floor of the valley like a bug.

The force of the deceleration mid-flight had almost caused him to throw up. As he'd swallowed down the bile flooding his throat, the demon goddess had spoken to him.

"I've been waiting for you, son of Samyaza."

To this day, Astarte still hadn't explained the meaning of her greeting. Nor had she remarked upon what his shield had done when he'd told her what had happened after Belial captured him, though he sensed she knew the reason the weapon had acted that way. Instead, Astarte had made him promise not to change into his dark angel form while they were down here and had requested that he go on a journey with her through the Underworld.

Left with little choice but to trust the fallen goddess, Drake had agreed to her demand. They'd started out immediately after he'd recovered from his sudden and dramatic relocation to Hell and hadn't stopped since except to eat and rest. Drake suspected Astarte didn't actually need to sleep and only paused their travel out of concern for him.

He'd only questioned her intentions once. Her reply had stunned him about as much as the fact that she'd been the one to save him in the first place.

"We killed your lover, so why are you helping me?" Drake had asked her quietly that first night in Hell. "You had every reason to let me fall to my death."

Astarte's crimson gaze had become unfocused as she stared across the canyon from the mouth of the cave they'd sought shelter in, seeing something he would never see.

"Travis's death was more my fault than it was yours," she had said finally. "You were only defending yourselves." A sad smile had curved her fiendish mouth. "It is not rare for a high demon to maintain an attachment to someone he or she cared for before they fell to Hell. And it is unsurprising that that pure, selfless emotion gets twisted into lust in the Underworld. After all, sex is one of the ways in which we demons can replenish our dark powers. But it is exceptional for a helldragon to be granted his human form again so he can mate with his commander."

The goddess's eyes had found Drake then. In their depths, he had read agony and a loss he would never be able to fathom.

"Hellbeasts were once divine beings and humans that we angels had fallen in love with. And the oath that bound me to Belial had everything to do with the man I had given my heart to when I was still a goddess. He followed me to Hell when I fell, even though it meant his body would be transformed into that of a monster."

Her voice had trembled slightly as she paused for breath.

Surprise had run through Drake. *The hellbeasts were once heavenly beings and humans?!*

"Belial was the one who made Travis human again," Astarte had continued in a lifeless tone. "I don't regret asking him to do it. It gave me centuries of memories with the one I love. Memories that will stay with me for an eternity." Her expression had turned grim. "But now that

Travis is gone, my oath to Belial has been fulfilled and I am the mistress of my own fate once more."

"What was his real name?"

Astarte's pupils had flared at Drake's question. It had taken a while before she'd spoken again. "Travis's name was...Ishiem."

A lull had fallen while Drake had digested her shocking confession.

"Does this mean you're one of the demons who wishes to defy Satanael?" he had said hesitantly. "Even though you are part of Hell's Council?"

Astarte's expression had darkened briefly with anger.

"Hell's Council is nothing but a gentlemen's club for fallen angels who should know better!" she had replied in a sibilant hiss. "Satanael and the Princes of Hell have long forgotten why we are down here and the reason our once heavenly forms were changed into these grotesque appearances." She had indicated her dark skin and claws. "Our time in the Underworld was meant for us to repent our sins and to grow into beings He could be proud to welcome into Heaven once more. Instead, Satanael wages war on mankind. His blackened soul remains full of hate and spite and he refuses to acknowledge the important place humanity holds in God's heart."

"Are you sure about that?" Drake had muttered. "Because, as far as I see it, humanity isn't doing that great for itself."

"Much of the evil that lurks in the heart of man stems from Hell's influence on Earth," Astarte had observed sedately. "I am not saying mankind is entirely blameless. They are just easily...persuaded. Like lambs being led to slaughter."

Drake settled presently on the bed of dead animal skins. Sleep did not come easy. Like all the nights since he'd arrived in the Underworld, his agitated dreams centered on that awful moment when he'd cut off Artemus's wing. The look of utter betrayal in his twin's eyes as he watched Drake fall into Hell in a shower of his own hot blood and feathers was one that still made Drake's chest tighten with regret.

At some point in the night, he woke up and took out the lone, white feather that had somehow wedged inside his clothes during his descent into the Underworld. The color had faded to pale ash and the quill was cold. Still, Drake found it comforting to hold. It was a connection he very much needed to his brother now that they were so far apart.

CHAPTER FOURTEEN

THE LAST WORDS DRAKE HAD SAID TO ARTEMUS WERE still on his mind when he stirred several hours later. He sat up, dragged a hand down his stubbled face to wipe the sleep from his eyes, and went to join the demon guarding the entrance of the cave.

"You should have woken me up."

Astarte didn't reply. Drake followed her unblinking gaze.

The place in which they'd sought refuge yesterday was located in a barren, cavernous space the size of L.A. Its ceiling was lost in hazy clouds of condensed sulfur and a river meandered through its desolate valley, the sinuous shape glittering in the pale twilight that bathed the Underworld.

Drake stiffened when he saw the distant outline of a vessel carving through the dark water and the procession of spectral shapes walking its banks.

"Is that...Charon's boat and the Styx?!"

"If by that you mean the guide for the souls of the

damned and his gateway, then yes." Astarte paused.
"There are many Styxes and Charons in the Underworld.
He is just one of them." She narrowed her eyes. "Although
it is unusual for the soulguides to venture this deep into
Hell."

Unease coiled through Drake as he gazed upon the pale
forms following the boat and the river. "So, the dead do
end up here."

"Yes. They make tasty snacks for demons and
hellbeasts."

Drake felt the blood drain from his face.

Astarte's low chuckle rang in his ears. "I'm kidding.
Dead people's souls taste terrible."

Drake bit back a sigh. Astarte's jokes were almost as
bad as Artemus's. He kept pace with the demon as she
headed into the valley, her loyal contingent of fiends
keeping a respectful distance behind them.

The rest of their day passed peacefully enough,
although Astarte's alert expression told Drake they were
never far from danger. She'd warned him the first night
he'd arrived here that Satanael and the rest of Hell's
Council would not rest until they'd scoured every corner of
the Underworld to find him. As the key to the seventh
gate, he was an invaluable resource they could not afford to
lose.

It was the reason she had warned him not to transform
into his dark angel mode. If he did, Astarte believed
Samyaza would be able to detect his location.

Even now, Drake could feel a faint tug in his gut where
Samyaza's bond still dwelled. That they'd remained under
the enemy's radar for so long was due wholly to Astarte's
intimate knowledge of the dimension she had been

banished to and her skills as a warrior goddess, things Drake would eternally be grateful for.

And if it means buying more time for Artemus to come get me, then I'm all for skulking around in hidey holes.

That his twin would find a way to enter Hell and rescue him was not something Drake ever doubted. From what Solomon had said, doorways between Earth and the Underworld had the potential to exist at fractures between the dimensions. If there was a way out of the Underworld, then there was bound to be a way in. Artemus was the most stubborn person he knew. And Smokey and the other Guardians were just as bullheaded as he was.

Serena's face danced across his mind then. Drake's heart twisted painfully, just as it had done every single day since he'd been wrenched from her arms by Belial. That he'd not managed to say goodbye to her was something he would have to live with for the rest of his life, however short that could prove to be.

Drake's watch was reading five p.m. when they exited a twenty-mile-long tunnel that burrowed under several mountains and emerged into yet another rugged canyon. A river snaked along the barren landscape to their left, its path broadening as it carved through the bedrock in lazy twists and turns. It disappeared around a tall cliff in the distance, the low rumble of its rapids echoing against the walls of the gorge.

They rounded the bend a while later. Drake slowed, his eyes widening.

The gully had opened up to form a forested valley ringed by mist-wreathed peaks. A giant castle of bones towered at the far end, ahead of them. The rooftops of a city rose beyond the pale ramparts at its base, the river circling the defensive walls before disappearing through a low, wide watergate at the bottom of the palisade.

Though Drake had made out several such strongholds on the horizon in the past two weeks, it was his first time seeing one up close. The calcified human remains making up the facade of the palace and its defensive walls glowed dully in the gloom, as if radiating the life force that once dwelled within them. It was a grim reminder of where exactly he found himself.

Movement at the gates that provided the only access point into the demonic city drew his gaze. Drake tensed at the sight of the group of demons headed for them by air and on the backs of a pack of hellhounds.

"Stay behind me," Astarte warned. "These demons don't know you and fiends tend to talk with their claws and fangs first."

Drake obeyed the goddess and stepped into the shadow of her wings. To his surprise, she closed them around him, wrapping him in a warm, musty cocoon that masked his presence but still allowed him to see what was going on through faint gaps in the dark feathers.

Their party was soon surrounded by the city's guards. The ground trembled and angry noises filled the air as Astarte's demons and the new arrivals spat and hissed at one another, their rivalry clear to see. A voice boomed out a command to the sentries, halting their threatening moves toward Astarte's horde.

Dirt puffed up in a cloud as the head demon, a creature some ten feet tall and almost half as wide, dropped down from his hellhound and landed in front of Astarte. "My Goddess."

The earth shook under the impact. Drake staggered

slightly inside the shelter of Astarte's wings. To his surprise, the head demon lowered himself onto one knee and bowed his head respectfully to Astarte.

"Please pardon our discourteous welcome. I had no warning of your visit." He straightened, his mouth twisting in what passed for a demonic smile. "My lord will be pleased to see you."

"Thank you, Us'gorith," Astarte murmured. "I have brought a visitor to meet with him. Pray extend your hospitality to my guest as well as the fiends faithful to me."

Us'gorith's expression turned guarded as he studied Astarte. "Is he the one you protect with your wings, Goddess? The being who smells human and demon at the same time?"

Drake made a face where he hid behind Astarte. He should have remembered a demon's sense of smell outdid a human's by a mile.

Us'gorith's troop stirred with alarm at their leader's words. The hellhounds stamped their giant paws and growled as tension thickened the air.

"There is only one being who carries the scent I can taste in the air," Us'gorith continued. "And that is Samyaza's son."

CHAPTER FIFTEEN

"*Samyaza's son?!*"

The hissed cry rippled through the guards and brought about a wave of almost palpable fury. Drake clenched his jaw. These demons obviously loathed Samyaza.

"Understand one thing, fiends of Armaros," Astarte declared in a steely voice. "Samyaza's son is under my protection. And none here shall harm him, or you will taste my spear and my fangs."

Drake blinked, more than a little stunned and wondering at the oddly familiar name she had spoken. Never in a million years could he have imagined the situation he found himself in right now, in the midst of Hell with a fallen goddess coming to his defense against her own kind. He came to a decision.

"It's okay, Astarte."

Astarte frowned as Drake dipped out from beneath the wall of feathers keeping him safe. He stepped up to her side and tilted his head to meet Us'gorith's ochre gaze, his own unflinching despite his racing heart.

"I may be Samyaza's son by virtue of my birth but his claim to me ends there. I am not my father."

Rumbles erupted amidst the crowd of scowling demons surrounding them.

"Your lord will want to see him," Astarte told Us'gorith.

The head demon held her gaze for a moment longer before raising a hand and silencing his irate troop. The hellhounds whined in disappointment when they realized they would not be tasting their enemy's blood today.

"Very well," Us'gorith said in a forbidding tone. "Let us see what my liege has to say on this matter. But if I sense any threat from Samyaza's heir, I shall carve his head from his body myself."

This won the head demon a rousing cheer from the guards. Drake sighed.

Yeah, like I could threaten any of them in my present form.

Dozens of suspicious demonic stares probed his back as they were escorted toward the city of bones. They crossed a drawbridge spanning the river and entered the outskirts of the metropolis through its towering gates. Drake looked around curiously as they started up a central thoroughfare.

The place resembled an ancient, medieval human town. Buildings made from mud, wood, and stone rose around him, open windows bright with the glow of the cooking fires that burned in their hearths. Demons going about their daily business meandered the streets, some moving in pairs and small groups, as if they were family.

Drake was stunned to see children among them.

It wasn't long before they came upon what looked to be a manufacturing district crowding the embankments of one of the canals that crisscrossed the city. Drake spotted smithies and shop stalls lining cramped passages through the fumes spouting from the smokestacks dotting the roofs of factories and warehouses.

The roads widened as they approached the palace, the houses and buildings they passed more detailed in their architecture and constructed of bones. They navigated another drawbridge and crossed through a pair of thick gates before finally entering the palace grounds.

Drake tensed. Their escort had brought them to a stop on the edge of an immense, sunken, granite courtyard accessed by a set of shallow steps.

A giant, black helldragon lay some thirty feet to the left of where they stood. The beast was feasting on six skewered hellboars cooking above a firepit, claws scraping meat lazily off bone as he chewed and swallowed, his expression somewhat bored. Opposite him and to the right, a demon with deadly curved horns tipped with hellfire hammered at a red-hot blade with a frown of concentration, the forge burning brightly behind him casting flickering, orange light over his imposing frame.

"My liege, you have guests," Us'gorith announced.

The dragon and the demon looked their way. They froze when they registered Astarte and Drake's presence.

Drake startled as his watch transformed into the shield. "What the—?!"

He sagged sideways, the weapon dragging his arm down until it thudded pointed edge first into the ground.

Astarte stared. "I wondered if that would happen. It seems it remembers its makers after all."

The horned demon's crimson eyes widened. "My shield!"

The dragon dropped his hellboars into the fire in surprise and clambered to his feet. "My scale!"

The demon and the dragon dashed toward Drake.

"Er, Astarte?" Drake mumbled as the ground shuddered beneath them.

"Don't worry. Armaros and Vannog won't harm you. Besides, if I'm right, they'll soon—"

A thunderous noise boomed across the courtyard as the demon and the dragon crashed into one another in their haste to get to Drake. They cursed and fell to the ground.

"—do that," the goddess finished with a hint of disdain.

"Hey, that's *my* shield!" Armaros barked at the dragon as he leapt to his feet.

"Oh really?!" Vannog hissed. He scrambled to his clawed feet and circled the demon, his barbed tail carving the air threateningly. "Well, that's *my* scale. I made it with *my* body! All you did was shape it into a weapon and mutter some spells, you foolish angel!"

Drake blinked as he finally recalled where he'd seen the demon lord's name. It had been in one of the books from Sebastian's arcane library.

Armaros is the Eleventh Leader of the Grigori. He was the angel named the Accursed One!

He stared at his shield, his pulse pounding. "Wait. This is a helldragon's scale?!"

The weapon shifted back into a watch. Drake touched it hesitantly.

Astarte glanced at him with a frown. "Vannog was a divine beast before he became a helldragon. His hide was one of the strongest things in Heaven."

Us'gorith sighed heavily as the air filled with seething accusations, Armaros and Vannog shoving viciously at one another while they argued. The rest of their fiendish escort erupted into loud cheers and urged the dragon and their demon lord on. From Us'gorith's long-suffering expression, Drake had the feeling this was a regular thing.

Astarte's frown deepened into a scowl.

"For Christ's sake, will you two cut it out?" she barked. "You're giving me a headache!"

Us'gorith sucked in air. His guards gasped, their shocked expressions clearly indicating Astarte had uttered what passed for blasphemy in the Underworld. The warring dragon and demon paused before slowly stepping away from each other, their faces projecting haughty innocence.

"I see you still have a foul mouth, Astarte," Armaros said with a loud sniff.

"Indeed she does." The dragon's pupils dilated as he gazed curiously past Astarte. "Where is Ishiem? I do not smell him."

Astarte stiffened briefly. Drake's fingers curled into fists, guilt arrowing through his heart all over again.

"Ishiem is dead," the goddess said quietly.

Shocked mumbles erupted from Us'gorith's guards.

Vannog's eyes rounded. Armaros frowned.

"Come," the demon lord murmured. "It seems we have much to discuss."

He turned and led the way into his palace of bones.

CHAPTER SIXTEEN

GIDEON MORGAN'S COMPOUND WAS LOCATED SOME forty miles southwest of Santa Ana, in a mountainous valley of the Sonora Desert accessible only by helicopter and all-terrain vehicle, in Mexico. The sun was low on the horizon when the convoy of 4x4s carrying them to their destination finally entered the canyon providing the only surface access to the reclusive genius's home and research facility. The dirt road they were traveling along was soon replaced by smooth blacktop.

Artemus pushed his sunglasses up onto his head as the lead vehicle turned a corner. He studied the complex of interlinked structures cascading down the hillside and across a rocky shelf up ahead with a faint frown.

The buildings had been designed to blend into their surroundings, the hard lines of their concrete, glass, and steel components softened by limestone, granite, and greenery. Artemus knew from Serena's description that the official headquarters of the team of mercenary super soldiers she and Nate once belonged to extended deep inside the mountain. From what Lou had implied, the underlying superstructure would survive a nuclear explosion.

The road twisted up the hill and ended in an immense, paved, circular driveway overlooking the valley. Artemus stepped out of the vehicle he'd been riding in with Smokey, Sebastian, Otis, and Lou. He gazed at the glorious sunset bathing the landscape in hues of red and orange. Despite the harsh desert environment, the valley was beautiful.

The other 4x4s piled up behind them and unloaded the remaining Guardians as well as Serena, Nate, Tom, and the rest of their team.

"Pretty, isn't it?" someone said behind Artemus.

Artemus twisted on his heels. A man had appeared from out of the main house.

Artemus frowned. He hadn't heard the stranger approach. He glanced at the open doorway behind Gideon Morgan before focusing on him.

Standing five foot eight, the super soldier looked to be the same age as Tom and sported a shock of jet-black hair, cobalt-blue eyes, and a pleasant if reserved smile. But it wasn't his face that drew Artemus and the Guardians' stares and sent surprise shooting through them.

Gideon was wearing an exoskeleton to walk.

Artemus didn't doubt that nanorobots had been used in the technology.

Gideon smiled faintly, clearly registering their undisguised astonishment. "The legs always freak people out at first."

"I'm sorry. We didn't mean to stare," Callie murmured awkwardly.

Jacob clutched Daniel's hand, his expression wary.

"It's okay, kid," Lou said. "He doesn't bite. Well, not in that sense."

His eyes sparkled as he smiled at Gideon. He closed the distance to the super soldier, tilted his chin up gently with a knuckle, and kissed him.

Artemus and the other Guardians' eyes rounded. Wolf-whistles echoed around the valley as several super soldiers put their fingers to their lips. Serena and Nate gaped.

"They're a couple?" Serena asked Tom.

Tom rubbed the back of his neck, a happy grin on his face. "Yeah, Lou finally gathered his nerve and asked him out."

"Asked him out, wooed him with a homemade dinner, and promptly ravished him, all in one week," a female super soldier said with a chuckle.

"I'm not surprised," Serena muttered acerbically. "He's been wanting to ravish him for ten years."

"What does ravish mean?" Jacob asked innocently.

"You are too young to know what that is yet," Daniel said firmly.

"Oh, come on, the kid was killing demons a couple of days ago." Tom raised a finger and leaned conspiratorially toward Jacob. "It's when two people get naked and—*ouch!*"

Serena had slapped him sharply on the back of the head.

"Hey!" Tom looked at Serena with a wounded expression. "What was that for?"

Jacob wrinkled his nose. "Oh. Do you mean sex?"

Callie's mouth fell open. "How do you—?"

"I read a book in Sebastian's library the other night," Jacob said with a hint of pride. "It was called the Kama Sutra. It had pictures." He made a face. "Gross ones."

The rest of them stared at Sebastian.

"I am not his babysitter," the Sphinx said with a frown. "The library is open to everyone."

"Er, are they coming up for air?" Otis murmured, gazing at the still kissing pair.

Gideon's expression was slightly glazed when Lou lifted his mouth off his.

"I thought we agreed not to do that in public," he mumbled, his cheeks flushed.

Lou chuckled. "I missed you too."

Serena pointed an accusing finger at Gideon. "I can't believe you sent your new boyfriend after us. We could have killed him!"

"But you didn't," Gideon said mildly.

Serena's frown deepened.

"How about we all go in and have some food?" Gideon indicated the main house. "You must be tired after your travels."

The compound's interior was surprisingly pleasant despite its austere lines and large, uncluttered spaces. The furniture was functional yet attractive and a collection of modern art pieces that Artemus knew cost an arm and a leg dotted the bare, stone walls.

Gideon had obviously spent millions on the design of the place.

It wasn't until he saw Serena and Nate's old team disappearing throughout the complex with their duffel bags that Artemus realized it was their home.

"You guys all live together?" he asked Gideon curiously as the super soldier led them through the main house, his steps smooth despite the exoskeleton frame enclosing his legs.

"Yeah. The Immortals who rescued us from Greenland thought it best if we stayed close to one another." Gideon glanced at him. "We agreed. Besides, this place is big enough to house a hundred people and more."

Sebastian arched an eyebrow. "King and Greene helped you build this compound?"

"No," Lou replied. "Howard did."

"Who's Howard?" Leah asked.

Serena grimaced. "Howard Orson Rodney Titus. He's the CEO of STAEGH Corp. He's also an Immortal."

Haruki whistled softly under his breath. "*The* STAEGH Corp? As in, the top tech company in the world right now?"

"I have business dealings with them, but I've never met their CEO," Callie said.

"Same," Sebastian murmured.

"Trust me, you don't want to meet their CEO," Gideon grumbled. "He's a jackass."

Lou grinned. "He changed the wifi password to Hot Rod again, didn't he?"

"That moron is asking for a fight," Gideon said darkly.

"That moron gave us the money to build this place and taught you everything you know." Lou dropped a kiss on Gideon's head. "Although, he's learned a few tricks from you too, over the years."

"If the guy is an Immortal, it makes sense that he would stay out of the limelight," Haruki observed thoughtfully.

"The other two silent co-CEOs of STAEGH Corp are Immortals too." Serena hesitated. "They formed part of the main team who freed us."

They slowed as they entered a dining room. Artemus stared.

The place was big enough to be a restaurant and projected out over a sharp drop in the mountainside. Split on two levels, it afforded a dizzying view over the valley that led to the compound through three massive, thirty-foot-tall, glass walls and a transparent floor. Purple shadows were filling the ravine as the sun finally set. Stars popped into existence in the cloudless sky above the desert.

One of the two chefs manning the cooking station in the middle of the room looked up. His eyes brightened.

"Nate! Good to see you, buddy. Wait till you taste these ribs! It's gonna make you green with envy."

Nate smiled faintly. "Hi, Manuel."

"Is he a super soldier too?" Callie asked as Gideon led them to a table.

"No," Gideon replied. "Manuel and George are our live-in chefs and caretakers. They are half-breed Immortals."

Daniel startled. "You mean, like Persephone?"

Gideon blinked. "If you mean Pope DaSilva, then yes, I do."

The super soldiers who'd accompanied them from Chicago started filing into the dining room from other corridors, voices raised in easy conversation. Just like the unconventional household he was now host to, Artemus could tell the men and women gathering around him treated each other like family.

Dinner was a noisy and warm affair. To his surprise, Artemus found himself relaxing in Gideon and the other super soldiers' company. He grimaced into his wine.

And to think we were at each other's throats two days ago.

Artemus became aware of Gideon's watchful gaze. He

cleared his throat and asked the question he'd been dying to ask for a while.

"So, hmm, were you born this way or did the Immortals do something to you when you were a child?"

Leah sucked in air. Daniel and Otis let out weary sighs. Callie looked like she wanted to sink into the ground.

"Seriously, man," Haruki mumbled.

Sebastian scowled at Artemus before looking at Gideon with a contrite expression. "My most sincere apologies. My young friend here has no filters. We are still teaching him manners."

"Hey, if you're gonna blame anyone, blame those four for not warning us," Artemus protested.

He indicated Serena, Nate, Lou, and Tom.

Gideon put his knife and fork down. "I guess a disabled super soldier does come as a surprise." He met Artemus's eyes steadily. "The answer to your question is yes. To both. I was still a fetus when they damaged my legs, so it's not as if I felt a thing. They wanted to see if the nanorobots could repair developing tissue." A sad look flashed briefly in his eyes. "I was the only one who survived those particular experiments. The ones whose spines they severed didn't fare as well."

Lou reached across the table and took Gideon's hand.

Artemus frowned. "Did they make it out alive?"

Gideon stared. "Who?"

"The ones who created you," Artemus grated out.

"No," Serena said quietly. "The Immortal children who rescued us killed all of them."

"Good," Artemus said darkly.

It wasn't until they were having coffee that Gideon finally raised the issue of why they'd come to Mexico.

"Lou said you needed my help with something."

"Yes. It's two things, actually." Artemus hesitated. "First, I want you to find the seventh gate to Hell. Second, I need you to help me make a nanorobot wing."

Gideon's eyes widened.

CHAPTER SEVENTEEN

"Beel brought Nephilim to the surface?" Armaros said, horrified.

Drake nodded. "Yes. It started out as these strange earthquakes. A Nephil attacked Artemus in Chicago and another one killed the mayor a few days later." He frowned. "Rome was a whole other ballgame. Beelzebub brought an entire army of Nephilim to the Holy See."

Vannog huffed where he'd poked his head through the window of the castle. "So, that was what we sensed that time."

"Tremors," Armaros explained at Drake's puzzled look. "They are rare down here, and we don't normally pay them much heed. The ones we felt a few weeks ago were different."

Lines wrinkled Astarte's brow. "It was thanks to a new sword Michael's son made and Hydra's poison that they managed to overcome the Nephilim. That, and the seraph's growing powers."

Vannog hissed. "That venomous hag is still around?!"

Armaros rolled his eyes at the helldragon. "Just because Hydra beat you once doesn't make her a hag, Vann." His curious gaze shifted to Drake. "Your brother is a blacksmith?"

"Yes." Drake paused. "Probably the best one in the world judging by that sword."

"Oh." Excitement lit the demon lord's eyes. "I would love to meet him and see the weapon he made."

"You may soon get your chance," Drake muttered.

Armaros stared. "What do you mean?"

Drake shifted awkwardly under the demons' and the dragon's crimson gazes. Until now, he had deliberately omitted revealing to Astarte the full details of what had transpired between him and his twin in Rome before Belial dragged him into the Underworld.

"I, er, may have told Artemus to come find me in Hell."

Shocked silence followed. Astarte broke it.

"You what?!" the goddess growled, her voice booming around the room.

Fumes snorted out of Vannog's giant nostrils as the helldragon burst out laughing.

"Knowing Michael, his son is probably dull-witted enough to actually try it!" he chortled, wiping tears of merriment from his eyes.

"You asked your Guardian to come to the Underworld?" Armaros said, aghast.

Astarte rose and paced the room. "You realize if Satanael gets his hands on you *and* Artemus, it's game over, right?"

Judging from the way the goddess was fisting her hands, Drake had the feeling she was holding back the urge to wring his neck.

"Yes. But I also know he won't stop until he gets me back," he retorted stubbornly. "Besides, we promised each other, the night Alice died." His voice faltered. "We promised we would always be there for one another." He met the demon goddess's scowl unflinchingly. "If the situation were reversed, if Artemus were the key to the seventh gate and I the Guardian, you can be damn sure I would move Heaven and Earth to find him, even if it meant coming to the Underworld to do so."

A tense hush descended upon them in the wake of his statement.

Astarte gritted her fangs. "Goddamn brothers!"

Drake relaxed slightly at her expression. The goddess looked less inclined to tear him apart with her claws.

A loud crunch echoed around the room.

Vannog paused where he was munching on a hellboar.

"What?" the dragon said defensively in the face of Armaros and Astarte's pointed frowns. "All this chatter about fighting is making me hungry." He noted Drake's mildly interested air and daintily offered him a half-chewed leg. "Would you like some?"

"Er—"

Armaros sighed. "He would no doubt prefer one not covered in your disgusting saliva. Come, let's go find you some food."

Drake observed his surroundings guardedly while they navigated the wide palace corridors. Armaros's taste in decoration erred on the garish side. The heads of the numerous monsters he had felled were mounted on the bone walls alongside extensive weapon displays and the hides of rare beasts.

"If you're wondering about the human remains, they

weren't taken from living people," Astarte said. "They are what is left of those who have died over the millennia of human wars."

"The Underworld isn't exactly rife with building materials." Armaros grunted at Drake's surprised expression. "Besides, a bone castle is—what's that newfangled word? Oh, yes. Cool."

Astarte rolled her eyes hard. Drake smiled faintly.

The demon lord guided them to the basement of the palace and the kitchen and dining hall that took up half its space. To Drake's surprise, the chambers they entered wouldn't have looked out of place in an eleventh-century castle. Instead of damned souls, hellcreatures sizzled above giant roasting pits set in hearths lining the walls of the immense room, while others simmered and bubbled in vats above roaring fires sitting next to water wells. Demons scurried about in the hot, humid air swirling up to the vaulted ceiling, their hands busy with tasks Drake didn't care to take too close a look at.

"That's a lot of food," he observed as they settled at the head table in the dining hall.

"Helldragons are hungry beasts," Armaros said. "So are my troops."

As if on cue, the double doors at the end of the dining hall creaked open. A horde of rowdy demons filed in and headed for the long tables lining the floor in an orderly arrangement, Us'gorith the tallest among them.

Vannog trailed in behind the fiends, the entrance wide enough to accommodate his body, though he had to duck to clear the lintel. He nosed about in the kitchen, his long neck darting over to various pots and pits as he inspected their contents. The soft clicks he made in the back of his throat reminded Drake of a mother-in-law gauging the cooking of her son's new bride.

The dragon placed his order, waddled over to the hearth next to the head table, and plonked down in front of it. His eyes gleamed as he watched demon servants scurry over with his food.

Drake wasn't surprised to see that a third of what had been prepared had been intended for the helldragon.

Vannog ate it all in minutes, licked his chops clean, and let out a burp that rattled the tables and the bone chandeliers suspended from the ceiling.

"Pardon me," he murmured primly.

He curled up on himself like a cat and went to sleep. Soft snores soon reverberated around the dining hall. None of the demon guards seemed to mind as they dug into their meals.

Drake's stomach rumbled. A servant brought him an entire leg of hellboar sitting on a platter of steaming, roasted vegetables.

Armaros chuckled as he watched him eat with unconcealed enthusiasm. "We'll make a demon out of you yet."

Drake paused and grimaced. "Don't even joke about that."

It wasn't until they'd finished their meal and the dining hall was almost empty that Drake finally questioned Armaros about the watch.

"How did it end up with me?" He made a face. "I mean, I get that Samyaza gave me his sword for some reason, but—"

"Samyaza didn't give you his sword," Astarte interrupted.

Surprise jolted Drake. "What?"

"Your father didn't bestow his sword on you," Armaros affirmed with a grim nod. "I stole it from him and hid it on Earth, just like the archangels did the various weapons they intended to grant to the divine beasts they'd chosen to wield them."

"Samyaza's sword appeared before you the night your powers first manifested, like it was meant to," Astarte said. "As did Armaros's shield."

Drake gazed wide-eyed at the demons, mouth dry. "But —*how*?! Why did you—?"

"Because we do not approve of Satanael's plans for our future," the demon goddess said with a frown.

"The two of us have no wish to fight humankind and our brothers who still stand beside Him." Armaros gazed steadily at Drake. "I was Heaven's most talented black-smith. I made all the weapons wielded by the archangels and the Grigori, including your father's blade and Michael's sword. As for the shield, it was the last thing I created before I fell to Hell."

Drake's pulse thumped as he digested this shocking information. He stared at his watch and looked searchingly at Armaros after a short silence.

"The thing it did when Belial dragged me into Hell— where it transformed into a sphere and broke his hold? Was that of your making?"

The demon lord beamed, fangs gleaming in the light of the nearby fire. "Yes. It was a spell I put on the weapon in case you ever ended up down here. Vannog was very pleased with how it turned out when we trialed it."

The dragon blinked a lazy eye open at the mention of his name, yawned, and settled back down, his breath rumbling steadily in and out of his nostrils in thin trails of smoke.

"He'll grow fat if you just let him eat and sleep like that," Astarte muttered to Armaros.

"Worry about your own hips, woman," Vannog said sleepily.

Astarte grumbled something under her breath and downed her drink. "By the way, I spotted something odd on our travels here."

Armaros narrowed his crimson eyes. "Odd how?"

"One of the soulguides. They don't normally come this deep into the Underworld." Astarte rubbed her chin thoughtfully with a hand. "It made me wonder if Hell's Council is making some kind of move."

A scowl darkened Armaros's face. "I wouldn't put anything past those fiends. The lot of them are a bunch of conniving, black-hearted devils!"

"They're probably looking for me," Drake said uneasily.

"Well, we can't be having that," Armaros grunted. A shrewd look dawned on his face as he studied Astarte. "We may have to play one of the cards we've been keeping up our sleeve."

Drake looked blankly between the two demons. "What card?"

Vannog woke up, smacked his lips, and gazed toward the kitchen with a hopeful gleam in his eyes. "Is it time for a snack yet?"

CHAPTER EIGHTEEN

SERENA STUDIED THE DATA FILLING THE DISPLAY TABLE IN the bunker that housed the compound's computer super-complex. She walked around slowly and tapped several of the images.

The spinning, holographic projections of several molecular compounds materialized above the liquid-crystal, holographic touchscreen.

"This is the analysis of the soil samples you and Nate sent me from those quake sites where the Nephilim appeared," Gideon said briskly where he stood at the head of the table. "The smell you guys detected was a combination of ozone and sulfur." He swiped the air with a hand. The holograms Serena had brought up vanished, only to be replaced by a host of others. "As for the rest of the dirt specimens' composition, I detected traces of radioactive materials when I ran them through the mass spectrometer."

Serena narrowed her eyes.

Artemus stared at the colorful structures rotating

above the table, his unease plain to see. "Wait. You're saying the Nephilim could be a source of radioactive contamination?!"

Gideon shrugged. "Possibly. Since I don't have a Nephil at hand to analyze, all I can tell you right now is the places where they appeared bear identical chemical signatures. But the radioactive elements I detected aren't enough to cause harm to humans, if that's what you're worried about."

Serena pursed her lips. Daniel closed his eyes and heaved a sigh of relief.

With the number of Nephilim who'd invaded Rome and the Holy See, no one wanted to suddenly discover the place had been ground zero of a nuclear event for two weeks and counting.

Sebastian frowned at the holograms of the radioactive compounds. "You believe this can lead us to the seventh gate?"

Serena heard the undertone of doubt lacing his words and couldn't exactly blame him.

"Maybe." Gideon's eyes glittered as he waved a vague hand at the information before them. "Look, I don't know much about Heaven and Hell, and the mystical powers you guys possess, but I know my science. The fact that these radionuclides were present at every location where Nephilim were sighted has to mean something."

"Solomon mentioned that the gate probably exists on an interdimensional fracture between our two worlds," Otis murmured.

"He also said it would likely be somewhere deep underground," Haruki added.

Callie looked nervously at Artemus. "Are you sure

about this? That you want to open the seventh gate to go find Drake?"

Smokey huffed anxiously, no doubt sensing the tension between them.

Serena bit her lip. It wasn't the first time in the last few days that the other Guardians had questioned the foolhardy plan Artemus had presented to them when they were still in Chicago. She and Smokey were the only ones who'd never doubted the angel's strategy. She masked a grimace.

But then again, we're biased, just like Artemus is.

"I agree with my sister," Sebastian said quietly. "Maybe we should reconsider. It is an incredibly risky move and one that could bring about the downfall of humanity. We must not make this decision lightly."

Serena sensed the other Guardians' disquiet once more across the bond that linked them.

"Don't you think it's about time you told them?" Otis murmured to Artemus, his tone mildly accusing.

Puzzlement shone in Daniel's eyes. "Told us what?"

"He's not planning to open the gate to go get Drake." Otis sighed. "He wants to use it to get *out* of Hell, with an army waiting to force it closed again."

"Bingo," Artemus murmured.

There was an audible intake of air all around the room.

"What?!" Callie mumbled.

Serena's pulse accelerated as she gazed at Artemus, understanding slowly dawning. *Oh. I see.*

Artemus made a face. "Solomon said it himself. There is only one thing that can open the seventh gate before the true End of Days. That's the power of the seventh key and its Guardians. I strongly doubt we're gonna be able to smash our way through it by human means, even if the blood of a goddess does run through my veins."

"Then, how the heck were you planning to go to the Underworld in the first place?!" Leah squealed.

"Chicago," Artemus replied confidently.

Haruki blinked. "Huh?"

"Wait." Sebastian scowled. "Is that why you asked Otis and me to put up a barrier at the auction house when we were on our way back from Rome?!"

Gideon stared. "You mean Elton LeBlanc's place?"

Artemus dipped his chin. "Yes. The breach where that Nephil appeared is still there. I told Elton to leave it unsealed since I suspected there might be an interdimensional fracture beneath it."

"Even if your supposition is correct, how the devil are you proposing we open it?!" Sebastian snapped. "I thought Ariton told Serena the Council of Hell was controlling all the portals in the Underworld!"

His voice echoed around the bunker. Tense silence ensued.

"You did it once, remember?" Artemus said quietly.

Sebastian looked at him blankly.

"London," Nate murmured.

"That's right." Haruki's eyes widened. "You opened a rift through Hell to find Drake that time he followed Amaymon and Serena to the Outer Hebrides!"

"And you found him because of the bond that linked him to Smokey and me." Artemus walked over to Sebastian and laid a hand on his shoulder, his expression resolute. "You are the Sphinx and the only Guardian with the power to manipulate divine energy. Hell is but an extension of Heaven. I *know* you can open a portal to the Underworld."

Sebastian's eyes darkened at his words.

"But I won't go until we have an exit point. One we can shut behind us." Artemus grimaced. "The last thing I want to do is spend eternity with that bastard Belial."

Gideon observed them steadily. "Well, the only clue we have right now is these soil samples. Like I said, I believe the location of a fixed gate of Hell will likely bear the same chemical pattern, unlike the ones attached to the artefacts and the Guardians who possess them."

"Where do we start looking?" Lou asked.

Gideon hesitated. "About that. Some people I know contributed to this data. Their resources outdo mine, so we should talk to them about identifying potential sites of a similar nature."

Serena stiffened. "Please tell me you didn't ask the guy I'm thinking you asked for help?"

Gideon's smartband chimed with an incoming call. He avoided Serena's accusing eyes and looked at the screen. "Speak of the devil."

His fingers danced over the display as he put the call through the main supercomputer.

The holographic projection of a dark-haired man with brown eyes appeared above the table. He looked to be in his late twenties, was sporting an MIT T-shirt that claimed geeks ruled, and appeared to be somewhere that looked remarkably like Gideon's bunker.

The stranger gazed curiously around the chamber. "Sorry, I didn't realize you had guests."

Lou grimaced. "Great. Another irritating Immortal asshole shows his face."

The stranger squinted. "Oh, hey, Lou. Wow, you've aged."

Lou flipped the Immortal the finger.

"Everyone, this is Jordan Banks," Gideon said curtly. "Jordan, this is everyone."

Banks grinned at his clipped tone. "Why do I get the feeling you're still pissed Eva beat you at your last VR game?"

"Who's Eva?" Leah hissed to no one in particular.

"She's the first fully cognitive AI in the world," Serena said grimly. "And Jordan is the one who created her."

"I'm not pissed at Eva," Gideon growled.

"Yeah, you are," Serena muttered.

A surprisingly melodious, computerized, female voice came over the speakers. "Good morning, Gideon. I am sorry my thrashing you at Hitman 20 caused you distress. We can have a rematch at your convenience, but I fear I will only defeat you again."

"Is that Eva?" Callie murmured.

Nate dipped his chin. "Yes."

Gideon glared at Banks. "Is that sarcasm? Did you teach her to mock people?"

"I didn't teach her anything," the Immortal admitted without a trace of remorse. "She learned it all by herself."

"I can also do disdain and contempt," Eva added helpfully. A pause followed. "How fascinating. The readings I am getting from your guests are quite unique."

"Readings?" Artemus said, puzzled.

"She can analyze our vitals and body language," Serena said in a disgusted voice.

"Hi, Serena," Eva said. "I must say, the nanorobots I can sense within you and Nate are generating some very unusual electrical activity."

Artemus narrowed his eyes. "She can detect divine energy?"

"Is that what it is?" Eva said.

"Yes," Artemus said, still suspicious.

"How very intriguing." Eva paused. "I cannot make out the physical or chemical composition of the power I can perceive in you, but the rest of your data is pretty plain to decipher."

"What does she mean by that?" Daniel said.

"For instance, it is clear from Mr. Kuroda's hormone levels that he wishes to mate with the young lady next to him," Eva stated blithely.

"Hey!" Haruki protested.

Leah gazed at the Yakuza heir with an expectant expression.

Haruki frowned. "I said not before you graduate from college. Besides, your father will shoot me if we have sex before you're twenty."

Leah sagged. "You're such a prude."

Haruki scowled at Banks. "And how the heck does she know who I am?!"

"Eva has access to pretty much every digital database in the world," Lou said acerbically. "She probably even knows what brand of underwear you're wearing."

Leah perked up in interest.

Jacob tugged on Callie's hand. "What's a prude?"

CHAPTER NINETEEN

Artemus stared at the metal tray on the table next to the anvil. A dark, silvery liquid filled it to the brim, the content glimmering as it moved sinuously. The plates making up his wing sat next to it.

"Are these the nanorobots?"

"Yes," Gideon replied. "They are in a dormant state."

Now that Sebastian knew the exact physical location of the super soldiers' compound, he'd been able to create a rift from there to Artemus's workshop in Chicago. Lou and Nate had helped him fetch the tools Artemus would need to make a new wing before the three of them had left late that morning with the other Guardians.

They were travelling in small groups to the locations Eva and Gideon had identified as potential sites for the seventh gate. All were known for having been the setting for a nuclear experiment or explosion. There were no new places Eva and Gideon had identified with unexplained radioactive readings that might indicate they were concealing a gate to Hell.

Only Smokey, Serena, Otis, and Jacob had stayed back at the compound with Artemus.

"Are you ready?" Gideon said.

He stood holding a tablet controlling three cameras able to track and record the chemical and electrical readings from the nanorobots.

Artemus took a deep breath and nodded. Flames exploded on his gauntlet as the weapon extended and enclosed his hand and wrist.

"Whoa," Gideon murmured.

Artemus stepped up to the anvil, dipped his fingers in the liquid-nanorobot medium, and applied it to one of the wing plates.

Gideon guided him as he slowly started working the two alien elements, the cameras providing a way for the super soldier to identify where best to place the artificial nanomachines.

Jacob perched on a stool a short distance away with Smokey on his lap, his mesmerized gaze locked on Artemus's fire-wreathed hands, the plate of cookies and glass of milk at his side all but forgotten.

The hours slowly ticked by. Perspiration soon dotted Artemus's face despite the air conditioning keeping the room at a cool sixty degrees.

The nanorobots felt more alive than anything he'd ever worked with before. It was taking every ounce of his metal-smithing skills to make them adhere to the components he'd created in Chicago.

It was evening by the time he finished coating the plates with the new, shiny layer binding them together. He wiped sweat from his brow and observed the end result of his hard work with a thrill of satisfaction.

"Want to test it right now?" Gideon said, unable to mask his excitement.

"It'll be better if we do it outside." Artemus shifted into his angel form and effortlessly picked up the wing. "There's not enough headroom in here."

They took the elevator to the first floor of the complex, Jacob blinking sleepily between them.

"You should get dinner and go to bed," Artemus told him.

Jacob rubbed his eyes and shook his head. "No. I wanna see."

Smokey huffed his accord.

Artemus sighed. "I don't know where the two of you get your stubborn streak from."

Gideon arched an incredulous eyebrow at him.

Artemus frowned. "What?"

Serena and Otis joined them when they exited the elevator. They made for one of the compound's internal courtyards, some super soldiers trailing in their wake.

Gideon and Serena helped Artemus place the new design on his back, the coated metal gleaming under the moonlight bathing the canyon. They stepped away as Artemus slowly flexed his wings to get the hang of how his new one felt.

Impressed murmurs rose from the group of super soldiers watching him.

Hope filled Artemus. Though the artificial appendage moved differently from his natural wing, he sensed he could control it. He flexed and extended it a couple more times before leaping into the air.

The metal wing held for all of ten seconds before falling apart, just like it had done in Chicago.

"Shit!"

Artemus braced his remaining wing to stabilize his hover. The people on the ground jumped back as the plates twisted through the air and clattered noisily into the center of the courtyard. Frustration twisted Artemus's belly as the nanomachines he had spent arduous hours fixing to the individual pieces slowly sloughed off the metal surfaces and pooled onto bare stone.

Artemus landed awkwardly next to them. "I really thought it would work this time."

He squatted and dipped a finger in the silver liquid. The nanorobots dripped off his skin and fell back into the puddle.

Gideon frowned. "It should have, technically."

"Why don't you two get some rest and try again in the morning?" Serena suggested. "It's getting late. Jacob needs to eat and go to bed."

"No, I don't," Jacob protested.

"You're literally sleeping on your feet, kid," Serena chided gently.

"Okay," Artemus said reluctantly while Jacob uttered another weak objection. "We'll try again tomorrow."

He frowned at the pieces of the wing and the silent nanorobots on the ground. *What am I doing wrong?*

"WE SHOULD GO ON A FORMAL DINNER DATE WHEN THIS is over," Leah said.

Haruki stared at her, surprised. Sand shifted beneath their feet as they navigated the Jornada del Muerto desert, in New Mexico. The super soldiers who'd brought them there followed a few steps behind them, wary gazes observing their surroundings through their augmented, night-vision goggles.

Haruki didn't need the device. He could see everything clearly without it.

They were in the middle of the Trinity Site, a restricted military zone inside the White Sands Missile Range. It was where the U.S. had tested its first nuclear weapon, in 1945. Though no Nephilim had been sighted near that location, Eva and Gideon had nonetheless pinpointed it as an area of interest.

Unbeknown to the rest of the world, the real Trinity Site was actually twenty miles west of the memorial that had been erected at a fake locale open to the public and tourists. It had taken Gideon a couple of hours that morning to get them temporary access to the regulated area.

The Geiger counter device strapped to Haruki's left wrist beeped, indicating they'd entered a region of increased radioactivity. The lip of a shallow crater emerged up ahead, under the starlight bathing the barren landscape.

"Any particular reason for the dinner date?"

Leah narrowed her hazel eyes at him. "Do I need one?"

"Er, no," Haruki murmured hastily.

"I turn twenty in four months. We should start practicing for the big night."

Haruki's pulse spiked as various scenarios flashed across his mind's eye, not all of them innocent. "Hmm, practicing what, exactly?"

"Having dinner at a high-end place." Leah glanced at him. "I know glamorous parties are something you're used to as the heir to the Kuroda Group, but I'm not. I'm an average girl from Chicago without a fortune to her name."

"Your grandmother is one of the richest women in the city," Haruki observed.

"She doesn't throw glitzy social functions," Leah retorted.

Haruki mulled this over. Though he would never admit this to her, he wanted nothing more than to make Leah his. But his orthodox upbringing and his respect for the woman he intended to marry one day, not to mention for her conservative father, meant he couldn't just follow his base instincts. It was why he'd been so careful for them not to do anything more intimate than kissing since they started going out. Not that they'd had much opportunity for dating since they'd gotten together.

Although Haruki's reputation in L.A. signaled him as a notorious playboy with a string of broken hearts behind him, the reality couldn't have been further from the truth. He could count on the fingers of one hand how many lovers had graced his bed since he'd left his home to go to Stanford. His brother Yashiro had even teased him about being too picky.

The real ladies' man in the family had been his easy-going, charming, older brother. Whereas Yashiro would often come home smelling of expensive perfume and boasting lipstick on his collar, Haruki had been the one who'd slinked in at dawn with bloodied fists and a black eye.

As usual, thinking about Yashiro brought a twinge to Haruki's heart. *He would have liked Leah.* He made a face. *Probably would have flirted with her too, just to wind me up.*

Warm fingers twined with his. Haruki looked down at Leah where she hugged his side.

"What are you thinking about?" she said quietly.

Haruki smiled faintly. He wasn't surprised she'd sensed the change in his mood. "My brother. The two of you would have gotten along well."

Leah was quiet for a while. "Mom would have liked you too."

Haruki squeezed her hand lightly.

"FYI, I think we should book a hotel for our first night together," Leah stated. "I get the feeling I'm going to be louder than Callie when we have sex."

Haruki tripped on his feet.

"Jesus Christ," one of the super soldiers muttered behind them. "Just get a room, will ya?"

CALLIE SURFACED FROM THE LUKEWARM OCEAN WITH Nate. She pushed her goggles up over the skin of her scuba diving suit and eyed the islands surrounding the lagoon where they floated.

Several clusters of light broke the gloom of a low land mass to the east. One of them was centered around the faint outline of the Runit Dome, the four-hundred-feet-wide, concrete capsule enclosing the radioactive debris from the nuclear experiments carried out on the Enewetak Atoll by the U.S. government during the middle of the previous century.

"We're almost out of time," Nate said.

Callie glanced at the vessel behind them and the armed men and women manning its deck. Their super soldier escort was indistinguishable in the gloom where they stood amidst the military team monitoring their activities.

"I know. One last dive and I think we're done." She smiled at Nate. "You ready, big guy?"

Nate pressed a kiss to her lips that made her toes curl. "Always."

"I HATE RUSSIA," TOM STATED GLUMLY.

"Technically speaking, we're above the Arctic Ocean," Daniel murmured.

Tom shivered and pulled his bomber jacket tight around his body. "It's still bloody Russia. And it's cold. I hate the cold."

"Will you stop bitching?" a female super soldier murmured. "You should be able to adjust your core temperature, like the rest of us."

"I don't wanna," Tom said petulantly.

"Let's just shoot him," another super soldier suggested.

Daniel swallowed a sigh. He'd forgotten how chatty the super soldiers could be. He looked out of the window of the Sikorsky Seahawk at the island growing to the west.

They'd landed in northern Russia just after midnight and had boarded the military helicopter that had been waiting at the airport in Amderma to take them to the archipelago of Novaya Zemlya.

Made up of two large, uninhabited isles sandwiched between the Barents and Kara Seas, the place had hosted most of Russia's nuclear testing programs since the Cold War, including the Tsar Bomba, the world's biggest thermonuclear weapon. They were currently headed for its test site on the southwest of Severny Island.

That they hadn't been intercepted by the Russian air force yet was a miracle Daniel put down to the super soldiers' use of advanced radar technology. Even so, they wouldn't be able to hide their presence from the hostile troops based at the testing site for long.

"Landing zone coming up in five minutes," a voice warned in the headset strapped to his ears a short while later.

Daniel took a deep breath as the helicopter started a steady descent toward their target.

CHAPTER TWENTY

SEBASTIAN SQUINTED AT THE SHAPE LOOMING OUT OF THE blizzard ahead of them. "Is that it?"

"Yeah!" Lou shouted.

The winds howled around them, buffeting their bodies and the snowbike in violent, unceasing gusts. The squall had appeared out of nowhere, just after they'd landed at the westernmost tip of the restricted area. It had brought with it shrapnel-like ice that stung exposed skin and heavy blusters that rendered them blind and deaf. If Sebastian had been a superstitious man, he would have divined that something didn't want them there.

The wall of ice and rock grew clearer as they approached it. Though he had heard the story of how it had been formed from Serena and more recently from Lou on the plane ride here, it was still an awe-inspiring sight to behold.

It had been twenty-two years since four nuclear explosions had rocked this uninhabited part of Greenland. Three of them had detonated deep underground, obliter-

ating the secret facility created by the Immortal pure-
bloods who had been experimenting on their own kind and
humans for decades with the aim of creating an advanced
breed of Immortals and the super soldier race that would
help them conquer the world.

The fourth device had gone off above ground and had
been intended to eradicate all life in a thirty-mile radius of
its location, including the enemies of the scientists and
Immortals who had stormed the place to stop their inhu-
mane research.

The explosion never accomplished its intent. Instead,
its destructive effects were stopped by the elemental and
psychokinetic powers wielded by two Immortal children.
The result of their incredible feat was a one-mile dome of
ice and rock that still stood to this day, in defiance of all
scientific explanation.

The outline of an opening drifted in and out of view at
the base of the western wall of the structure. Though
Sebastian had half expected the place to be heavily
guarded, it seemed the accord the Immortals had reached
with the U.N. Security Council was still in effect. No
human or Immortal had been allowed within a fifty-mile
radius of the place since the incident that occurred two
decades ago. Sebastian mulled this fact over as Lou slowed
their snowbike to a stop in front of the gateway.

*Gideon must have cashed in some heavy favors to get us access
to this place.*

The whine of engines rose on the wind as their super
soldier escort caught up with them. The men and women
dismounted from their vehicles, weapons in hand. Though
he couldn't see their faces behind their ski masks and
goggles, Sebastian sensed they were nervous.

This was the place of their creation, after all.

"We go on foot from here," Lou said curtly.

He led the way through the arch.

The silence that greeted them beyond the threshold of the dome was sudden and all the more shocking for being unexpected. For a moment, Sebastian thought the blizzard that had been raging across the land had stopped. He paused and looked over his shoulder.

The squall was a virtual whiteout where it raged outside the structure some ten feet from where he stood. Yet, no sound reached him. Sebastian pushed his goggles up on his head and peeled his ski mask down. He frowned, his breath pluming in front of his face. He flexed his fingers slightly and cast a weak pulse of divine energy toward the dome's pale walls.

The shield of sheer power it bounced off made his heartbeat accelerate. *There is more to this place than I initially thought.*

"You coming?" Lou called out ahead of him.

Sebastian registered the tension in the man's face and the stiff set of his shoulders as they resumed their trek.

Lou was one of the super soldiers old enough to remember what had transpired the night he and his kind had been rescued by the Immortals and their allies. The scars it had left were evidently still fresh in his mind, despite the passage of two decades. Still, Sebastian knew a day would come when the super soldier's trauma would eventually be assuaged.

Snow and ice crunched under their boots as they advanced toward the center of the dome. The landscape was unnaturally smooth and even, a result of the powerful forces that had stormed across it all those years past. They were a fifth of the way inside the structure when Sebastian pulled back the sleeve of his suit and checked the Geiger smartband on his wrist.

There was no trace of radiation whatsoever around them. He made a face.

Another physical improbability that cannot be explained by science.

Though this location contained none of the trace radioactive elements that Gideon's analysis had detected in the soil samples recovered from the sites where Nephilim had appeared, he had still suggested it as a place for them to investigate. The super soldier and Eva had argued the point for some time the night before. In the end, the super soldier's logic had won out.

"My gut is telling me we should check it out," Gideon had said adamantly. "Besides, that place is...unique. It would be stupid of us to ignore it as a potential location of the gate."

A crater took shape up ahead. They stopped on the edge and gazed down a steep slope to the chasm that occupied its center.

"How close do you need to get to detect a doorway to Hell?" Lou said.

"Closer than we are right now," Sebastian replied.

Lou sighed. "I was afraid you'd say that." He turned to his team. "You guys form a perimeter around us. I'll go down there with him." He paused. "If you see anything suspicious, shoot first and ask questions later."

"Do you mean demons or humans?" a super soldier murmured uneasily. He saw Lou's expression. "Never mind."

Lou drove a couple of spikes into the ice, secured

climbing ropes with belay devices to them, and clipped the ends to his and Sebastian's harnesses.

Gravity did most of the work for them as they rappelled down the incline of the basin. They reached the bottom after a couple of minutes and made their way over the icy ground to the closest lip of the thousand-foot-wide pit in the middle.

Sebastian lowered himself to one knee and peered into the abyss. It arrowed down smoothly, growing narrower after a hundred feet or so. Darkness filled its depths.

He wondered if the subterranean chambers the nuclear explosions had formed still existed somewhere deep below.

Only one way to find out.

Sebastian raised a hand and sent a blast of divine power out into the void.

CHAPTER TWENTY-ONE

Drake leaned over the bone parapet and gazed out restlessly over Armaros's realm.

It was past three a.m. and he couldn't sleep.

The woody smell of cooking fires imbuing the air had long since faded and the glowing windows dotting the demonic city had grown dark after its denizens had retired for the night. Only the flaming torches atop the defensive walls and those that marked the streets and waterways punctuated the soft twilight. High above, swathes of glow worms moved across the roof of the cavern, bright constellations that sparkled and glittered in an inky firmament of stone.

"They're not as pretty as real stars, but they are still something beautiful to behold, down here, in this place of eternal gloom," someone said behind him.

Drake looked over his shoulder.

Astarte strolled across the hall and joined him on the palace terrace. "Can't sleep?"

"No." Drake looked out over the slumbering city.

"There are many beautiful things in the Underworld," he said after a while. "It is not at all like the infernal place of fire, brimstone, and damnation described in religious texts." He grimaced. "Persephone would have a heart attack if she ever came down here."

A wry smile curved Astarte's mouth as she rested against the bone balustrade next to him. "I never thought I would live to see the day humans would elect a woman as the supreme pontiff of the Catholic Church."

"From what I heard, it wasn't exactly a straightforward nomination," Drake muttered.

"Well, chauvinism is as old as the world. You wouldn't believe the grief Eve got for what that stupid serpent did to her."

A comfortable silence settled between them.

"So, you really think Hell is pretty?" Astarte said with an undertone of doubt.

"Well, some of the aesthetic leaves something to be desired." Drake made a face as he indicated the bone castle behind them. "But, everywhere I look in this city, I see beauty." His tone turned pensive. "The demons who dwell here are nothing like the fiends who've attacked us on Earth. And it says a lot about you and Armaros that the ones loyal to you can lead such peaceful lives in a place that should be defined by hopelessness."

"You are a wise man, son of Samyaza," Astarte said after a moment.

Drake grunted. "I know a few people who would argue otherwise. One of them is going to talk my head off when he finds me. I already sense a headache coming on."

"May I take a look at it?" Astarte murmured.

Drake gave her a puzzled look.

"The feather you carry with you."

Drake stared. "You know about that?"

"It smells of your brother."

Drake hesitated before removing the faded quill from inside his shirt and passing it over to Astarte. She examined it for a moment before bringing it close to her lips. A frown of concentration marred her brow.

Drake's eyes widened when he saw the flash of gold in her scarlet pupils.

Astarte breathed out a pale, sparkling mist. It wrapped around the feather. The quill visibly brightened, its plumes almost glowing with vitality once more.

"How did you do that?" Drake mumbled as the demon returned the precious article to him.

The feather felt warm to the touch, as if it still bore the heat of his brother's body.

"You forget I was once a goddess," Astarte said with a sad smile.

A wave of emotion clogged Drake's throat at the unexpected act of kindness. He clutched the feather with gentle fingers.

"Thank you," he said shakily.

Astarte dipped her chin slightly. "It's a pleasure." She pretended not to notice the tears in his eyes and turned to observe the demon city. "It is a miracle that this place can sustain life. That we have water and food to keep us alive. It is all His doing, of course. And though the war Michael and his army brought to us was long and brutal, we could tell how much it cost our former brothers in arms to wound and slay us."

The goddess sighed. "I don't understand why that fool Satanael and Hell's Council do not see that it could have been so much worse. It was well within God's powers to kill us all." She snapped her fingers. "That's all it would have taken to banish us to eternal darkness. A click of his fingers. But He didn't. Because we are His children, warts and all."

"Michael told Persephone something when we were in Rome," Drake murmured, the poignant words Astarte had voiced sinking into him. "He said that the End of Days isn't just about mankind's redemption, but also about your absolution. And that he could never deny you the chance to redeem yourselves in His eyes."

"He is right." Astarte sighed. "Which is saying something for that stupid angel."

Drake chuckled. A thought came to him then.

"I saw children, when we first came to the city." He faltered, wondering if his next words would offend the goddess. "I didn't know demons could procreate."

To his relief, Astarte didn't seem to mind the question.

"It's the reason we were banished to Hell in the first place," she told him wryly. "We could not control the hot urges of our loins. The Nephilim are proof of that." Her expression sobered. "It's not as if we are all fertile, though. Many demon babies perish in the wombs of their mothers."

Her fingers clenched on the parapet.

Drake stayed silent, sensing the intense sorrow radiating from the goddess at his side. Remorse flooded him all over again at the thought of the man she had loved and that he had helped kill.

A sudden heaviness swamped the air. The hairs rose on Drake's arms. He straightened, skin prickling and hands squeezing the bone balustrade

He knew this pressure.

Motion beyond the city walls drew his gaze. Astarte swore beside him as several giant, crimson rifts burst into existence in the valley.

"Those fools!" the goddess hissed. Her viper-wreathed spear materialized in her right hand, the serpents hissing as they coiled around her wrist. "We told them to be subtle!" She frowned at Drake. "Come, you'll be safer with us than if you stay here!"

Drake's heart slammed against his ribs as he followed her. By the time they reached the palace courtyard, Armaros was already on Vannog and was busy securing two huge broadswords to the back of his demonic armor.

Astarte frowned up at the demon lord. "Can you sense it too?!"

Armaros nodded grimly. "Yes. There are demons in their party who do not belong here. I don't know what possessed them to bring those fiends to my realm!"

"Go with them," Astarte ordered Drake curtly.

Before Drake could ask what was going on, the goddess extended her dark wings and shot up into the air. Horns boomed across the city, the guards manning the walls sounding the alarm.

Drake gasped as Vannog curled his tail around his body and lifted him none too gently onto his back. His stomach lurched as the helldragon broke into a gallop. Drake almost fell off the beast. He grabbed Armaros's waist and clung on with a white-knuckled grip, the helldragon's scaly hide digging into his legs.

The castle gates loomed ahead of them.

"Er, Armaros?" Drake shouted above the din of

Vannog's pounding feet. "We're gonna crash into those if we don't slow down!"

"We won't," the demon lord said confidently.

Thunder clapped behind Drake. A burst of wind whipped at his clothes. He looked over his shoulder. His eyes widened.

Giant, black wings soared out from Vannog's back. The helldragon flapped them once and rose, his claws glancing off the top of the gates as he flew over them.

CHAPTER TWENTY-TWO

Vannog climbed fast for a beast his size. A cold gust pressed against Drake's face as he peered down the helldragon's curved body. The city blew past them in a flash, the buildings looking like miniature doll houses far below. They crossed the river and were soon over the plains.

Tears sprung to Drake's eyes as he squinted past Armaros to the hellish portals growing ahead of them. His belly twisted at the sight of the vast and terrible army pouring out of the rifts.

Shit. That's a lot of demons!

Us'gorith and Armaros's troops were already aligned a hundred feet or so from the swarm of ochre-eyed fiends and monsters when Vannog landed behind them seconds later.

Astarte alighted some way ahead, her figure oddly small against the solid wall of demons and hellbeasts looming above her. She folded her wings, strode to the middle of the no man's land separating her from the strangers, and slammed her spear violently into the ground.

"Why the hell are Satanael's followers with you?" she roared at the vanguard of five colossal demons sitting astride towering hellmonsters that could squash her at any moment. "And didn't we say you shouldn't travel here through the portals?! You've probably given our location away, you *cretins*!"

"Oh, dear," Armaros muttered. "She is on the war path."

Drake gaped. He could tell the demon figureheads and their hellbeasts were as powerful as Astarte, Armaros, and Vannog from the ruby glow of their pupils. He could also see their fierce expressions turning awkward in the face of Astarte's rage.

"I told you she would be vexed," one of the demons muttered to no one in particular.

Another demon cast a frown at him. "There were mitigating circumstances, Arakiel."

"Yes, well, you should know by now that that goddess over there doesn't give a flying angel about stuff like that, Chazaquiel," Arakiel said glumly, cocking a clawed thumb at Astarte. "She's all vim and vigor."

"These followers of Satanael and Hell's princes sought our protection," the third demon told Astarte calmly. "We could not turn them away."

"And what if they are spies, Tamiel?" Armaros jumped off Vannog's back, landed in the dirt with a loud thud, and shouldered his way past his troops to join Astarte. "This could very well be a ploy by that bastard serpent to infiltrate our armies!"

Drake's pulse raced as the names of the demons sank

into his consciousness. They were all Leaders of the Grigori.

Tamiel sighed. "You know as well as I do that I can detect deceit, Armaros. None can hide their true intentions from me. I have already examined these fiends' minds. They do not mean us harm."

The demons and hellbeasts behind the five leaders shuffled restlessly, ochre gazes wary as they glanced toward a spot in their midst. Drake could see a rough circle demarcating the fiends and monsters whose presence Astarte and Armaros objected to. The former minions of Satanael and Hell's Council huddled in the center of the horde, their faces full of fear.

The fourth demon slid off the back of his giant, horned, red helldragon and dusted off his armor. "If anything, they wish to join us in our fight."

He headed over to Armaros and pulled the demon lord into a quick bear hug.

"What about the portals?" Astarte challenged. "We told you not to use them, Zaqiel."

Drake stared at the Fifteenth Leader of the Grigori.

It was his prayer that Karl LeBlanc had inscribed on the gun he had made for Artemus, before his death. The gun that Michael had helped Karl put together without his express knowledge and that could vaporize demons and cast them back to Hell.

"We had no choice," the last demon said. "Satanael is moving his troops through the netherworld and we would have crossed paths with them had we taken the route you advised."

Astarte stiffened. Armaros frowned heavily.

"Is what Ramiel is saying the truth?" the goddess said

between gritted fangs as she looked from the fiend who'd spoken to the other four.

Tamiel dipped his chin solemnly. "It is."

"And the rest of our brethren in Hell Deep?" Astarte asked.

Tamiel shared a guarded glance with the other demons. "They are still making their minds up as to whether to assist us."

"Does that include Azazel?" Armaros said tensely.

"I fear Azazel may never join us, now or in the future, my friend." Zaqiel shook his head lightly, his expression sorrowful. "That demon has long lost his mind to grief."

Astarte and Armaros exchanged a troubled look in the fraught silence that followed.

Drake's pulse thumped rapidly. It was clear from the demons' expressions that the Third Leader of the Grigori, the fallen angel who had given rise to the race of witches and sorcerers who walked the Earth, was an ally they hated to lose.

Ramiel's gaze had locked on Drake. "Is that Samyaza's son?"

The demon extended his inky wings and alighted from his helltiger.

Drake tensed as the Sixth Leader of the Grigori headed toward him.

"He is smaller than I imagined," Arakiel murmured to Chazaquiel.

Zakiel rolled his crimson eyes. "Size is not everything, Arakiel."

Arakiel bristled. "Oh, really? Well, *you* would know!"

Tamiel cut his eyes to the two demons before they could trade further insults. Though he was the Fifth

Leader of the Grigori and technically outranked by Arakiel, Drake could tell the other fallen angels deferred to him to an extent.

Ramiel came to a hover beside Drake. "Tell me, is my spear alright?" he asked anxiously. "Does the Lion care for it well?"

Surprise jolted Drake. He'd forgotten Ramiel was the true owner of Leah's divine weapon. "Mmm, yeah, I guess."

Ramiel closed his scarlet eyes and pressed a hand to his chest. "Thank goodness." The demon heaved a sigh of relief. "I was worried that beast would scratch it with his claws. He is quite reckless, you know."

Drake thought it best not to tell the fallen angel that the Nemean Lion's host was an impulsive redhead who matched her beast for rashness. Movement among the leading rank of demons and hellbeasts distracted him.

Zaqiel's horned helldragon leaned down and nudged at something behind her left foreleg. "Go on. Say hello to your father."

Drake blinked. *Father?*

His eyes rounded as a small, purple, horned helldragon poked his head out from behind the hellbeast and stared at Vannog. A rumble of pleasure vibrated through Vannog's flanks. The black helldragon straightened and almost upended Drake onto the ground.

The baby helldragon darted out from his mother's side and made a beeline for Vannog. *"Papa!"*

Drake's jaw dropped. *Papa?!*

Armaros's demons parted hastily as the baby hell-dragon rolled into a cannonball and barged through their lines. He crashed into Vannog's foreleg with an *"Ooof,"* leapt to his feet, and shook his head dazedly. Sparks erupted from his nostrils as he sneezed out the dirt he'd inhaled.

Vannog leaned his long neck down to inspect the baby beast, soft purrs and clicks echoing in the back of his throat.

"Hello, little Vozgan." The helldragon poked his son lovingly with his snout and sent him tumbling to the ground once more. "You have grown much since I saw you last."

"Look! Look what I can do, Papa!"

The little helldragon clambered upright and inhaled deeply, his scaly cheeks swelling to the size of his head. A fireball as big as a bus burst from his jaws and scorched the ground in front of Vannog.

Drake blanched.

Vannog laughed, the sound booming across the valley and the reverberations shaking Drake's legs.

Vozgan's mother came forth to greet the black dragon. "I see you are well, Vannog."

Vannog lowered his head and raised his shoulders slightly, posture suddenly sheepish. "Hello, Isaya."

The female helldragon's pupils flared. "I hear you were cavorting with some sea serpents a while back." Her regal tone grew cool. "The hellbats in my realm were all too keen to report your affairs to me."

Armaros narrowed his eyes at Vannog. "Is that why you smelt of kelp that time you came home after going missing for a month?"

"Your dragon needs a chastity belt," Zaqiel muttered to Armaros.

Vannog ignored the demons.

"I cannot help it," he whined at Isaya. "My loins are full

of fire and must be unleashed regularly. It is a matter of survival, dearest."

"Please don't unleash anything while I'm sitting on top of you," Drake begged the dragon.

Isaya sniffed haughtily before blowing out smoke in Vannog's face. "My mating cycle will soon be upon me. You must visit me when that time comes."

Vannog's wings shivered against his flanks. "Oh."

Vozgan beamed where he stood between his parents. "I want two brothers and a sister!"

CHAPTER TWENTY-THREE

"GODDAMMIT!"

Artemus swiped a heavy hand across the table and knocked the metal components of the artificial wing to the floor. They landed noisily on the polished tiles, adding to his ire. He gripped the edge of a worktop and clenched his teeth hard against the wave of bitterness threatening to overwhelm him.

It was seven a.m. He'd been in Gideon's lab for three hours, sleep evading him for most of the night as he thought long and hard about how to fix the problem of getting the nanorobots to adhere to the wing elements. He knew it was the only way to make the structure malleable enough to endure the battle ahead and to give him a fighting chance against Hell's armies. Above all else, it was the only way he could save Drake. Yet, whatever he did, the wing would not work the way he could see it in his mind's eye.

The pneumatic hiss of the lab doors drew his irate gaze. Gideon and Serena strolled in, Leah tagging behind them with a tray of food and a coffee. She and Haruki had returned from New Mexico late last night. Callie, Nate, Daniel, and Tom had followed a few hours later, arriving at the compound early that morning. The only ones who hadn't come back from their trip yet were Sebastian and Lou.

Leah put the tray down on the worktop next to Artemus. "Here. Breakfast."

He scowled. "I'm not hungry."

Serena grabbed his arm, dragged him over to a stool, and forcibly sat him down.

"Eat," she snapped. "You look like hell. And you're not gonna achieve anything working on an empty stomach."

Gideon picked up the pieces of the wing and put them back on the table. "She's right."

Artemus grumbled under his breath, grabbed a fork, and jabbed a pancake. The headache that had been throbbing between his temples started to abate as sugar hit his bloodstream.

"Did Nate make these?" he grunted reluctantly.

"Yes." Leah smiled wryly. "And there's more where that came from, so you can wipe the drool from your mouth."

Artemus mumbled his thanks after he finished the meal, the coffee bringing another surge of much needed energy to his body. By then, Gideon had completed his analysis of the work he had done that morning.

Artemus joined him at the station where he sat, manning four supercomputers. "Any ideas?"

"Not really." Gideon frowned. "I sent yesterday's data to Eva. She couldn't think of anything we could have done differently."

Leah lifted a wing plate and turned it over in her hands.

"Maybe you're trying to mix two things that oppose one another."

"What do you mean?" Serena said.

"The nanorobots are sentient to an extent, right?" Leah said.

"Correct," Gideon replied with a curious frown.

"Then, maybe they don't like that they are being forced to work with these particular metals," Leah suggested.

Artemus sighed and raked his hair with a hand. "Are you saying I should make the wing elements with something else?"

"No." Leah shrugged. "I was just thinking of opposition and attraction in the theory of composition. It's a shame there's only one kind of nanorobot. I bet if you had something that complemented your powers, this might actually work."

"Well, I don't know where to—" Artemus started in a low grumble.

Something smashed onto the floor, startling them.

They all stared at Serena where she stood, her chair knocked to the ground behind her.

"What did you say?" the super soldier mumbled.

Leah exchanged a puzzled glance with Artemus and Gideon. "Mmm, I said if there was a type of nanorobot that mimicked Artemus's abilities, then this might—"

"My nanorobots." Serena's voice rose in excitement. "Use mine and Nate's nanorobots!"

Her eyes gleamed as she brought forth her powers, her skin erupting with a golden light. She clenched her fist and studied the eerie radiance bathing her fingers with a fierce expression.

"Your nanorobots are infused with divine energy," Artemus said hoarsely, his eyes rounding.

A grim smile curved Serena's lips. "Exactly."

"Holy shit," Gideon mumbled.

"WHERE IS EVERYONE?" LOU MUTTERED AS THEY navigated the super soldiers' compound.

"I can sense them somewhere out back," Sebastian said.

Lou glared at him. "And you! Why the hell didn't you rift us back here?"

"I needed the time to cogitate. Besides, you almost vomited when I took you to Chicago through a portal."

Lou looked at him blankly. "Cogitate?"

"Cogitate means to—" Sebastian started helpfully.

"I know what the hell cogitate means!" Lou snapped.

Sebastian kept quiet as they walked deeper into the complex, a trace of guilt darting through him. *I guess I should not have been as blunt as I was back there.*

He would never forget the look on Lou's face when he'd told him what he'd sensed at the bottom of the chasm in Greenland. The super soldier had gone pale before his face had twisted in a grimace.

"How ironic," he'd muttered. "And terribly fitting."

"So, what did you need to think about?" Lou grumbled presently.

"Our strategy going forward. Although Artemus has a plan for how we should proceed, it is far too crude for my liking. We need to be more tactical about our next steps."

Lou grunted. "And you needed eight hours of flight time to do this?"

Sebastian shrugged. "Yes."

Lou heaved a heavy sigh. They exited the compound and headed for a training amphitheater built into the side of the mountain, the sun low and dusk but a few hours away. The rest of the Guardians and super soldiers were already at the arena. Even Manuel and George, the two chefs, stood amongst them.

They were all staring upward.

Lou frowned at the sky. "What are they looking at?"

Sebastian's eyes widened, his preternatural gaze picking up more than the super soldier could detect. "Bloody hellfire."

"What?"

"He is at your two o'clock."

When the super soldier failed to get his meaning, Sebastian took hold of his head and gently moved it in the direction he'd indicated.

Lou's lips parted on a soft gasp of surprise.

Something glinted high up above them.

The dot grew into the shape of a winged man flying toward them at a dizzying speed.

Artemus landed in the middle of the arena with a thunderous sound that boomed across the valley. The stone cracked under his armored boots as the echoes died down, fractures radiating out from the point of impact. He straightened to his full height and looked over his shoulder at his artificial wing, a grin splitting his mouth.

Gideon's smartband pinged with an incoming message.

He glanced at it, did a double-take at what he read, and narrowed his eyes at Artemus. "How high did you go?"

Guilt danced across Artemus's face. "Hmm. Pretty high. Why?"

"Did you by any chance see a passenger airliner up there?" Gideon said grimly.

Artemus scratched his cheek and avoided the super soldier's scowl. "I, er, might have."

"There's no might about it!" Gideon barked. "Eva just sent me a picture someone uploaded to the internet thirty seconds ago. It's blurry as hell but she was able to identify your sorry ass flying past an aircraft headed for Mexico City!"

"Wow," Leah muttered. "Social media is scary."

"Amen," Haruki said.

"Gideon is so sexy when he's angry," Lou murmured to Sebastian. "It makes me want to rip his clothes off and—"

Gideon twisted on his heels and glowered at his lover, his ears reddening. "You realize we can all hear you, right?!"

"But it's true," Lou protested.

Sebastian headed over to Artemus, his curious gaze on the artificial wing on the angel's back. It took but seconds for him to discern the divine energy infusing the nanorobots welding the metal pieces together.

"This is a surprise," he murmured.

"It was Leah and Serena's idea." Relief darkened Artemus's eyes as he touched the wing. "It finally worked."

The other Guardians joined them.

"How does it feel?" Daniel said curiously.

"As good as new," Artemus gushed. "I can barely tell the difference between my real wing and this one."

Smokey made a pleased sound in Jacob's arms.

Artemus's expression sobered when he met Sebastian's eyes. "I take it you came upon something in Greenland?"

Sebastian arched an eyebrow. "How did you guess?"

"Because the rest of us didn't find anything at the other locations," Callie replied.

Sebastian exchanged a glance with Lou. "You are correct. There is something in Greenland."

"What did you find?" Otis said stiffly.

"Evil."

CHAPTER TWENTY-FOUR

VOZGAN STARED AT DRAKE. "IS HE A HUMAN?"

"Yes," Vannog said in an indulgent tone.

"Can I eat him?"

The baby helldragon sat up eagerly where he had been lying in the fold of his mother's tail, a bloodthirsty gleam in his eyes.

"No, child," Isaya murmured. "He is part demon too. Besides, he probably tastes like that spotted eel you hate."

She glanced at Drake, her expression apologetic.

Vozgan made a face. "Eels are yucky."

He huffed out thin trails of smoke and lay back down.

Drake swallowed a sigh and leaned against Vannog's flank. He glanced at the tent where Astarte, Armaros, and the other demon lords were having yet another council of war. It had been four days since the Grigori leaders had arrived in Armaros's realm. They'd refused the demon lord's invitation to stay at his castle and had insisted on remaining with their armies on the valley plain.

Campfires dotted the ever-present twilight that bathed

the cavern. Us'gorith and his fiends had spent most of the
first two days carting over food and materials from the city
for their unexpected guests. A low drone of voices and
animal noises rumbled around Drake as demons and hellbeasts settled down for the evening in their temporary
home.

Though he'd wanted to participate in the discussions
Astarte and the Grigori leaders had been having for the
last three days, Armaros had insisted he stay at the castle.
Today was the first time the demon lord and Astarte had
requested that he accompany them to the campsite. Drake
was wondering why they'd left him sitting outside for so
long and whether he should risk barging in there when a
hand parted the tent's opening.

Astarte stepped out and found Drake with her crimson
gaze. "Come."

A bout of nerves danced through Drake as he climbed
to his feet and headed over. He took a shallow breath. The
decisions being made by the demons could affect his future
and potentially that of mankind, and he damn well
deserved to have a say in them.

Arakiel greeted him with a sneer the moment he
entered the tent. "I cannot believe you asked the son of
that foolish angel to come to Hell."

Tamiel flashed a frown at the demon. "I thought we
said we were not going to attack him."

He went back to studying the faded maps spread out on
a table before him.

"I'm not attacking him," Arakiel retorted sullenly. "If I
were attacking him, my sword would be buried in his
heart."

Drake steeled himself under the demons' dispassionate

stares. "I cannot fall into Satanael's hands. And the only ones who can stop that from happening *and* get me out of Hell are my brother and Smokey."

"You don't seem to have much confidence in us, child," Chazaquiel grunted where he sat filing his claws, sparks rising with every scrape of stone against talon.

Drake folded his arms across his chest and arched an eyebrow, aware he was being brazen and not really caring. "Can any of *you* take me back to the surface?"

Zaqiel downed his drink, slammed his tankard on the table, and wiped his mouth with the back of his hand, his expression exasperated. "You know very well that all portals to your world were locked down tight after you arrived here."

"Probably that bastard Bel's work," Arakiel grumbled.

"Satanael evidently suspected some of us would offer you assistance," Ramiel mused. "Still, it was quite a risk to ask your Guardians to come here."

"If the situation were reversed, I would do the same for Artemus and Smokey."

"How do they intend to travel to the Underworld?" Tamiel indicated the ancient charts before him, his tone full of doubt. "Like Zaqiel said, all the portals are closed and their locations are likely being guarded by Satanael's troops."

Drake rubbed the back of his neck awkwardly. This fact had been weighing on his mind too.

"I think Artemus might use Sebastian's abilities to open a rift somewhere near my location. He managed it before, when the two of us got separated in England." He hesitated. "It was because of our bond."

Tamiel's expression remained dubious. "Alright, say the

Sphinx succeeds in doing that; how the devil do you intend to get out of here? The portal he creates will be a one-way route to the Underworld."

Drake carefully avoided Astarte's eyes. *Well, here goes nothing.*

"I suspect Artemus will use the, er, seventh gate."

A stunned hush followed his words.

"*WHAT?!*" Astarte roared.

Arakiel looked at Tamiel. "Did I hear that right? Did that idiot just say they intended to open the seventh gate?"

"Opening the seventh gate will unleash all of my and Artemus and Smokey's powers," Drake argued in the face of the demons' scowls. "Even though we are strong in our angel forms, I know we have yet to achieve our full potential, like the other Guardians have. It's the only way we will ever have a fighting chance against Satanael and Hell's Council."

Armaros grabbed Astarte under the arms and lifted her bodily off the ground as she tried to charge Drake. "Calm down, woman!"

"Let me punch him!" Astarte snarled, crimson eyes blazing with a deadly light. "I'll only break his jaw. I won't kill him, I swear!"

"You've really put the hellcat among the pigeons now," Ramiel muttered to Drake.

Drake grimaced.

The tent creaked ominously.

"What's going on?" a voice rumbled.

Vannog had poked an eye through the opening and was observing them curiously.

"Is everything alright?" Isaya asked anxiously in the distance.

"Yes, dearest. It's just another goddess on a rampage."

The helldragon disappeared.

"Put me down, Armaros!" Astarte said between gritted teeth.

"Only if you swear on Ishiem's name that you will not harm him."

Astarte stiffened.

"That's low, even for you," she growled at the demon over her shoulder.

"Sometimes, you just have to play dirty," Armaros retorted stubbornly.

Astarte took a shuddering breath. "Alright, I promise not to hurt him."

Armaros put her down carefully.

"Are you insane?!" The goddess shrugged his hands off and walked up to Drake, practically spitting in his face. "You will literally give Satanael what he has always wished for!"

"We won't." Drake clenched his jaw. "I swear."

They stared at one another, neither budging in the tense silence that befell them. Their deadlock was broken by the sound of an alarm. The air trembled with a sudden wave of corruption. Astarte's eyes widened. Drake's pulse spiked. Shouts rose outside.

He followed the demons as they stormed out of the tent.

"They've found us," Armaros growled.

Dread twisted Drake's gut at the sight of the rift taking shape a quarter of a mile away. Panic swept the camp as fiends and hellbeasts alike registered the impending arrival of their enemies.

A demon wearing a golden crown came out of the

portal atop a mammoth-like hellbeast, disdain pasted across his cruel face.

Tamiel narrowed his eyes. "Oriens."

An enormous fiend sporting armor made of stone followed the demon prince on the back of a giant, scarlet, horned helldragon.

"Balmon!" Isaya hissed, her crimson pupils flaring as she glared at the hellbeast.

Vozgan peered out fearfully from behind his mother's leg. "Is that Uncle?"

"Yes." Vannog saw Isaya's expression and butted her flank gently with his head. "Fear not, dearest. I shall not let your brother harm you."

Arakiel scowled. "It seems that bastard Turiel has chosen his side."

Drake's mouth went dry as he gazed at the figure in stone armor. Turiel was the Eighteenth Leader of the Grigori, the one known as the Mountain of God. An army twice the size of the forces of the demon lords presently gathered in Armaros's realm appeared behind the two fallen angels.

CHAPTER TWENTY-FIVE

"PLEASE, I'M BEGGING YOU," ELTON PLEADED. "THIS IS insane!"

"I'm going, Elton."

Artemus ignored the guilt storming through him as he watched his oldest friend's face crumple. He knew Karl was at the forefront of Elton's mind right now, as was the promise Elton had made to his dead brother two months ago.

"I know I said I wouldn't oppose your plans before, but I absolutely forbid you from setting foot in Hell!" Persephone snapped where she sat clutching a cooling cup of tea at the table.

Daniel glanced between Persephone and Artemus, clearly torn. "Mother."

Nate wordlessly replaced Persephone's drink with a hot one.

"Thank you," she murmured, her irate gaze moving briefly from Artemus.

Artemus raked his hair with his fingers and blew out a tired sigh.

They'd returned to Chicago late that afternoon, only to find Persephone and Elton waiting for them. An entourage of Vatican guards and police officers were currently encamped on the LeBlanc estate. Artemus had spotted Rossi among them. The Vatican cop had been their escort when they'd first gone to Rome in the summer and been attacked by Paimon's spirit cloud. He'd been eyeing the gravestones in the mansion grounds warily, the infamous tale of the undead reviving having evidently reached his ears through the Vatican grapevine.

"I have to rescue Drake from Hell before Satanael gets his hands on him," Artemus repeated.

"And if you fail?" Anger replaced the hurt in Elton's eyes. "Have you even thought of the consequences? What it could mean for the rest of mankind?!"

Artemus's hands clenched on the worktop he was leaning against. He chose his next words carefully.

"What if I told you that this was meant to be? That all of it was preordained, to a certain extent?"

Elton and Persephone looked at him blankly. Otis stirred where he sat on the window seat, Smokey on his lap. The seraph was frowning.

Artemus waved a hand vaguely in the direction of his assistant. "And I don't mean Catherine Boone's journals."

"What *do* you mean?" Persephone asked suspiciously.

"The girl in my dreams. The one I started seeing the night I met Smokey and inherited Michael's sword." Artemus gazed at them steadily. "What if I told you that she's shown me visions of what is to come? That I've seen flashes of the future through her on a few occasions now?"

Otis's eyes widened, as did Nate, Daniel, and Smokey's. Persephone grew still.

"What girl in your dreams?" Elton said, confused.

Artemus swallowed a sigh. The only ones he'd told about the woman he secretly loved were his brother and the other Guardians. And he'd only given them brief details at that.

Elton grew pale as Artemus recounted how he'd first dreamed of her when she was but a child, like him. How she had helped him unleash his angelic powers in that back alley where he'd been ambushed by gang members, just before Karl found him. How she had grown into a woman he had come to cherish dearly over the last two decades of dreaming about her.

"She was the one who showed me a glimpse of the gauntlets I made in Rome." Artemus registered Daniel's shock with a wry grimace. "And she came to me the night the Nephil attacked us in Chicago." He paused, the memory of what had come to pass still raw in his consciousness. "I saw it." Artemus swallowed convulsively as he met their stunned gazes. "I saw Drake fall to Hell. And I also saw us fighting Hell's Council in front of the seventh gate."

A deafening silence befell them.

Persephone clasped her cup tightly, her gaze unfocused and her expression strangely resigned. "I see."

"Mother?" Daniel said anxiously.

Persephone seemed to come to a decision. She studied Artemus with a faint frown. "If that's the case, then we can't stop you."

"What?" Elton scowled. "Visions be damned! We can't just let him go to Hell!"

Persephone stretched an arm across the table and covered his hand with her own. "We have to. If *she* saw them in Hell, then it will happen, whatever we do."

Artemus straightened, his heart thumping. "You know who she is, don't you?"

Persephone sighed. "I won't lie to you. But I *will* tell you that I cannot speak of her. Not yet, anyway." She looked at him unflinchingly. "I suspect you will meet her soon."

Artemus was about to ask her what she meant by that when Serena walked into the kitchen ahead of Haruki, Leah, Callie, and Jacob.

"It's almost time," the super soldier said briskly.

Artemus stared. "What the heck are those?"

Haruki glanced at the utility belts and harnesses he, Leah, and Jacob wore. "Gideon made them for us before we left Mexico."

"He used the same material the super soldiers' combat suits are made of," Leah added helpfully.

"You are divine beasts!" Artemus snapped. "You'll tear through those in a matter of seconds!"

Haruki grinned. "No, we won't. He modified them for our use. Besides, they're handy for our new weapons."

He indicated the sheathed sword on his back and the guns strapped to his thighs.

"Is that a rocket-propelled grenade launcher on Jacob's back?" Elton said, horrified.

"Hydra likes it," Jacob said defensively. "If we infuse the bomb with our poison, it will do untold damage to the enemy."

"Dear Lord above," Persephone murmured.

The back door opened.

Sebastian walked in, the rift he'd used to return to the estate closing on the porch with a golden flash. "They're ready."

He cast something to Serena. She caught it mid-air and examined it closely. The object was flat and the size of a small coin.

Elton glanced at the second one Sebastian held. "What are those?"

"Transdimensional geolocation devices." Sebastian slipped his inside his pocket watch. "They should transmit our position at the seventh gate when we reach it from the other side."

"Transdimensional?" Elton repeated leadenly.

"They're still experimental." Serena put the device in her pocket. "Gideon made them while Artemus was forging our weapons."

Artemus looked at his hands and flexed his fingers slightly, surprised they weren't aching after the last three days.

He still recalled Gideon's shocked expression the night they'd finally gotten the artificial wing to work. After Sebastian had revealed the Immortals' defunct research facility in Greenland to be the likely location of the seventh gate, he had given Gideon an inventory of items to procure.

Gideon had perused the articles he'd listed with a frown while they headed to the dining hall. "That's a lot of metal and rare elements. It's gonna cost a pretty penny." He'd arched an eyebrow at Sebastian. "What do you need these for?"

Sebastian had indicated Artemus. "He is going to make weapons for you and our allies."

"Huh?" Artemus had mumbled.

Sebastian had glanced at the super soldiers filing into the room around them. "I have given this a lot of thought. I believe our initial plan was lacking something. There is a chance Satanael and Belial might send demons to Greenland to stop the rest of you from providing us with assistance when we attempt to escape Hell." He'd observed Gideon steadily. "You do not stand much of a chance against them with the weapons currently at your disposal. Neither do the Vatican agents who will no doubt join you."

"What kind of weapons do you want him to make for us?" Lou had asked curiously.

"Ones that can slay demons and hellbeasts ten times more efficiently."

Tom had grinned. "I like the sound of that."

"Hmm." Artemus had rubbed his chin thoughtfully. "You're right. And I should modify their guns while I'm at it."

To Artemus's complete lack of surprise, the materials Sebastian had requested had been waiting for him in one of Gideon's workshops the next morning. He'd spent the following two and a half days forging scores of swords just like the one he'd created when Karl had briefly returned from his grave a couple of months ago. He'd also made adjustments to the super soldiers' firearms so they were nearly as powerful as Karl's gun at disposing of demons, even without Zaqiel's blessing.

"Dinner will be ready soon." Nate stirred a large pot at the cooking range. "I made everyone's favorite. Spaghetti and meatballs."

Serena frowned. "We're having dinner?"

"I thought it would be a nice thing to do before we leave," Artemus said defensively.

"Like the Last Supper?" Haruki shrugged at their expressions. "I'm just saying what we're all thinking."

"I shall not miss your lack of tact while I am in Hell, Dragon," Sebastian muttered.

Despite the nervous tension twisting everyone's guts, dinner was a resounding success. Persephone even had seconds and insisted on getting Nate's recipe for the attention of the Vatican's chefs.

It was past nine p.m. by the time they left the mansion. Persephone watched them leave from the gates of the estate, her expression guarded. Daniel stared at her longingly through the rear windshield of Nate's SUV until she disappeared from view.

It didn't take long for them to reach the auction house in Lincoln Park. Elton greeted the men and women guarding the property with somber nods as he led the way inside. The place had been closed to the public ever since the attack several weeks ago.

They headed toward the rear of the sprawling, brownstone mansion, the damage the Nephil had wreaked evident everywhere they looked. The barrier Otis and Sebastian had erected after their return from Rome danced warmly across their bodies when they passed through it.

The chasm in the center of the ballroom was still there. Cracks split most of the Corinthian columns holding up the ceiling and stars were visible through the giant, gaping hole above them. They navigated the mess of concrete, marble, and plaster in their path and stopped on the edge of the void.

Callie rose on her tiptoes and hugged Nate tightly. "This is it."

He tilted her chin with a knuckle and kissed her. "Be careful down there."

Callie smiled tremulously. "Right back at you." She turned and ruffled Jacob's hair gently. "Look after Nate."

Jacob sniffed and wiped his eyes on the sleeve of his jumper, his cheeks flushed. "I will." His voice changed to that of his divine beast. *"Kill lots of demons for us."*

Elton yanked Artemus into a bear hug. "Don't do anything stupid."

Artemus squeezed him tightly. "I won't." He drew back and glanced from Sebastian to the ballroom door. "Is Naomi coming?"

Sebastian's eyes flared white as he transformed into the Sphinx. "I already said my goodbyes."

Artemus shifted into his angel form, his new wing unfolding smoothly from his back. As he'd suspected, the divine-energy-infused nanorobots had been able to absorb the metal components into his skin, just like his regular wing. It meant he could unleash it at will, rather than having to rely on someone to put it on him.

He met Serena's gaze.

"You'd better not screw this up, Goldilocks," she said, her tone tense despite her relaxed face.

Artemus smiled faintly. "And you guys better be there."

He lifted Smokey into his hold in his rabbit form while Sebastian hoisted Callie into his arms.

"Don't drop me," Callie warned her brother as he rose above the chasm.

Sebastian sighed. "I am not like the butterfingered angel over there."

Smokey looked worried all of a sudden. He gripped Artemus's arm guard with his furry paws and clung on grimly. Artemus sighed and soared into the air.

He cast a final look at the Guardians and the super soldiers, the bond that tied them glowing brightly inside his soul. "See you in Greenland."

He tucked his wings and dove into the abyss after Sebastian.

Darkness swallowed them.

CHAPTER TWENTY-SIX

DRAKE CLENCHED HIS JAW AND CLUNG TO VANNOG SO hard his arms and thighs ached. His stomach dropped as the helldragon twisted through the air, sending the world spinning dizzyingly around them once more.

The hellbeast on their tail released a fireball that glanced harmlessly off Vannog's tail and missed Drake by some ten feet. The sulfurous blowback wafted across his face, bringing tears to his eyes. He blinked them away, not daring to let go of his ride.

A furious roar sounded at their back.

Drake squinted over his shoulder at the red helldragon chasing them.

Balmon looked just as pissed as the demon who sat atop him. Turiel's crimson eyes glowed hatefully as he glared at Drake, dark blood dripping down his left arm and flank where Astarte had injured him.

Drake looked at the valley below them and spotted the goddess where she fought the demons and hellbeasts who had dragged her to the plains.

Zaqiel appeared beside Drake. Astarte and the Grigori leaders had taken turns guarding him ever since the battle started, with Vannog helping to keep him out of Oriens and Turiel's reach.

"I really think I should change into my angel mode and help you guys!" Drake yelled above the wind. "Satanael and Hell's Council already know my location!"

"That would be foolish." Zaqiel slayed two winged demons with a lazy swing of his broadsword. "And trust me, if Satanael and Belial really knew where you were, all of Hell's armies would be here right now."

Another fireball skimmed past Drake's head.

"*You will pay for your betrayal, infidel!*" Turiel bellowed as he and Balmon gave chase.

Zaqiel frowned.

"Excuse me for a moment," he told Drake. "Vannog, if you would be so kind as to lend me your assistance."

He braced his wings and decelerated sharply. Vannog did the same. Drake bit back a groan as a startled Turiel and Balmon shot past on their right a second later.

These guys are hellbent on making me throw up!

Vannog accelerated again and clawed at Balmon's flank and tail. The red helldragon hissed in pain before banking away sharply.

It was all the opening Zaqiel needed to land a punch on Tamiel's face.

"Infidel implies I have betrayed a deity," he hissed at the stunned fiend. "Satanael is no god of mine!" He drew level with Vannog once more, a satisfied smile on his face. "I've always wanted to hit that smug bastard."

Arakiel materialized on Drake's left.

"Tag, you're it!" he shouted at Zakiel.

Zakiel nodded, tucked his wings, and plunged toward the valley.

The look Arakiel directed at Drake was more a sneer than a smile. "How're you holding up, kid? Have you been sick yet?"

Drake swallowed a sigh. *And this guy doesn't like me one bit.*

"No, I haven't been sick."

A distorted cacophony sounded behind them. Arakiel looked over his shoulder and narrowed his eyes at the demon prince on their tail.

Oriens scowled and winged his way rapidly toward them.

"Let's see if we can change that," Arakiel said.

Unease filled Drake at the Grigori leader's vicious smirk. Arakiel waved a hand. Drake's ears popped. Ripples blurred the air ahead in darkening, twisted waves. A whirling, inky vortex formed in Vannog's flight path. It grew exponentially.

Drake's breath caught. *Shit! Is that a—?!*

The helldragon beat his wings and gathered speed.

Drake gasped as the three of them were violently sucked into the black hole.

The valley vanished.

"ARE YOU SURE THIS IS THE RIGHT PLACE?"

Callie observed the tunnel they were navigating.

"I think so." A faint frown furrowed Sebastian's brow as he studied the gloom ahead. "I sensed Drake's energy coming from this direction."

Something wriggled inside Artemus's armor. He slipped a hand down his chest, grabbed the thing trapped within the body plates, and yanked it out. It was a fish with jagged teeth. Its eyes flashed ochre as it snapped its jaws at him.

He sighed, cast it aside, and dusted off his hands.

Smokey caught the creature mid-air and gobbled it down, his dark hellhound shape merging with the shadows around them.

Artemus grimaced before glancing at Sebastian. "You know, you said that the last time. Just before we ended up in that lake. With those sea serpents."

"Yes, well, it is not as if I possess the abilities of a guided missile," Sebastian said irritably in response to Artemus's faintly accusing tone. "Besides, it did not take long for us to stun those hellbeasts. And at least we *are* in Hell."

Callie shuddered. "You can say that again."

Artemus shared her sentiments.

Hell was vastly different from what any of them had expected it to be.

It had taken Sebastian half an hour to recreate the rift that had brought the first Nephil to Chicago. Though they'd all been able to sense the residual corruption left by the portal when they'd reached the bottom of the thousand-foot chasm beneath Elton's auction house, it had required all of Sebastian's concentration to uncover traces of Drake's energy beyond it through Artemus and Smokey's bond with their key.

Their journey to Hell had been long and tumultuous. Artemus had glimpsed scores of monstrous shapes in the distance as they'd flown through the hot, pulsing redness of the rift, the tortured screams of lost souls echoing in their ears and a sulfurous wind whipping at their bodies. Though it was their second time traveling through a demonic portal, it hadn't gotten any easier.

Their arrival in the Underworld had been sudden and wet.

Artemus's breath had locked in his throat when they'd emerged some hundred feet beneath a cold, murky lake. It had taken a moment for them to discern where the surface was, so clouded were the waters they floated in. By then, the creatures whose domain they had trespassed upon had appeared around them, giant bodies twisting in the shadows and creating eddies that would pull their prey deeper.

The look on the first sea serpent's face when Artemus had punched it in the snout had made Smokey snigger and accidentally swallow some water. By the time they had taken care of the hellbeasts and climbed onto the shore of the lake, the rabbit's fur had been clogged with the tiny, krill-like creatures that lived in it. He'd gotten rid of them by changing into his dark hellhound form and spraying out a shower as he shook himself dry, much to his brother's ire.

Sebastian had taken a moment to reorient himself before leading the way out of the cavern they'd found themselves in. The next one had been twice as big, with a ceiling wreathed in mist and a vast and forbidding forest covering the mountains that ringed it. In the end, they had decided to follow the winding river that cut through the valley in its center rather than venture beyond the treeline.

Though they remained on high alert, they did not come across anything more threatening than some hellrats and a group of weird, beaver-like creatures with horns busy building dams made from human and demon bones in the waterway. Bar the sound of rapids and the crunch of the remains that littered the riverbank, the silence was eerie.

The tunnel they had discovered on the other side of the cave burrowed underground for a considerable distance. A couple of hours had already passed since they'd entered it.

Artemus estimated they were about fifteen miles in when the ceiling gradually started to rise. The shadows began to lighten after another four miles. A faint, orange hue grew in the distance.

Smokey stopped several feet in front of them. He lowered his head and growled, hackles lifting.

The rest of them stiffened, weapons at the ready.

"What is it?" Sebastian asked the hellhound.

I smell hellfire up ahead. His ears flicked forward. *And I hear the sounds of a battle.*

Artemus's pulse accelerated. "Is it Drake?"

No. Smokey sniffed the air. He sounded surprised when he spoke next. *There are demons. Familiar ones.* The hellhound pawed the ground restlessly, eyes glowing crimson-gold. *But he is close!*

Artemus concentrated. His heart thumped with wild elation when he registered the faint energy signature Smokey had just detected.

"Try and keep up!"

He extended his wings, rose, and bolted down the tunnel.

Sebastian cursed and followed, Callie and Smokey racing beneath them at a dead run.

A low din reached Artemus's ears as he hurtled toward the lightening gloom. He unstrapped his swords and gripped them tightly. He soon made out the shouts and screams of demons and the clang of metal striking metal. The glow of fires filled the horizon, as well as a hazy twilight that heralded the end of the tunnel.

Artemus shot out into a canyon with towering, rugged cliffs. He slowed to a hover some thirty feet in the air and stared at the battlefield before him, not quite believing what he was seeing.

Sebastian caught up with him and halted abruptly by his side. "What the devil?!"

CHAPTER TWENTY-SEVEN

WIND RUSHED PAST DRAKE'S EARS AS THEY NAVIGATED an endless sea of cold darkness. A pinpoint of light appeared up ahead. It grew rapidly.

They bolted out of the black hole seconds later.

Drake cursed at the sight of the forest of giant ever-greens looming in front of them. The world tilted sicken-ingly as Vannog adjusted his flight path with a sharp twist of his enormous body and shot up above the treetops.

"Where the hell are we?!" Drake yelled once he was certain he wasn't going to throw up.

"In a cavern leagues from Armaros's realm." Arakiel gave him a dismissive glance as he kept pace with the hell-dragon. "It's one of several meeting points we agreed upon if we ever got separated."

Drake looked around at the mountainous valley unfolding beneath them. He clenched his jaw, frustration gnawing at him.

"We should go back and help them!"

Arakiel's expression grew stony. "Our priority is to keep

you out of Satanael's hands. Or have you forgotten that small fact?"

"I can't just let all those demons die at the hands of Hell's Council because of me!" Drake roared.

Arakiel's pupils flared in fury. "Well, you should have thought of that before you came down here. And why do you care for demons? You have killed plenty in your lifetime."

Guilt twisted Drake's gut, overcoming his anger for a moment. The face of Astarte's lover danced before his eyes.

"That was in self-defense and you know it!"

Vannog's body vanished beneath him.

It took a heartbeat for Drake to realize Arakiel had snatched him from the helldragon's back. The demon lifted him up by the neckline of his shirt, wings beating steadily in a hover as he half-choked him.

"Your selfishness and arrogance know no bounds, son of Samyaza!" Arakiel practically spat in Drake's face. "You waltz into Hell with no plans, destroy the fragile peace that has existed between factions of demons for millennia, and expect us to protect your sorry, privileged ass! And now you dare undo all our hard work on a *whim*?!"

Drake gripped the demon's wrist with both hands and glared at him, anger making his blood boil and stirring the evil that lived deep within him. "I didn't ask for any of this! I didn't *ask* for Samyaza to rape Alice! I didn't *ask* to be born with a demon eating at my soul!"

He leaned back sharply and headbutted Arakiel. Stars exploded in front of his eyes. The demon let out a surprised grunt.

"And it was Belial who brought me here, asshole!"

Drake snarled. "Maybe you guys should clean house before pointing fingers at others!"

Vannog appeared beside them.

"Er, Arakiel?" the helldragon said anxiously. "Maybe you should let him go. He's starting to turn the same color as Vozgan."

"Believe you me, I would love nothing more than to let this ungrateful mongrel fall to his death!" Arakiel hissed, rubbing at his forehead.

Drake was about to deliver a sharp riposte when something hot burst into life inside his chest, drowning out the sickening darkness that had started to consume his soul. He gasped.

"What's the matter?" Arakiel squinted suspiciously. "And why are your eyes glowing like that?"

Drake's heart raced as he recognized the divine power resonating with the power inside him. "He's here."

"Who's here?"

"Maybe he hurt his head," Vannog whined. "Astarte will be upset if you gave him a concussion."

"He's the one who thrust his skull in my face!" Arakiel snapped.

Drake's gaze focused on the distant wall to his right.

"Can't you feel it?" He grinned fiercely, startling the demon and the helldragon. "My brother. *He's here!*"

ARTEMUS CARVED TWO FIENDS' HEADS CLEAN OFF THEIR bodies, slashed another one across the belly, and kicked a fourth one in the groin. The demons cowering against the

cliff behind him whimpered, their arms wrapped protectively around their children. He frowned.

Drake's energy signature had grown weak. Neither he
nor Smokey could feel him as clearly as they had minutes
ago.

Flames erupted on his left, distracting him from his
grim thoughts.

Callie roared out a jet of fire that engulfed the demons
attacking a group of fiends and baby hellbeasts. Her spear
took care of those who escaped the blaze, the weapon
already coated with inky blood.

"Well, here's something I never thought we'd be doing
in this lifetime!" she shouted over.

Artemus swooped beneath a spiked club, elbowed the
demon who'd charged him in the face, and stabbed him in
the heart. "You mean defending demons?"

"Yeah!"

"They have children," Sebastian said grimly from the
air. "And they are not hostile toward us."

Artemus clenched his jaw. He didn't know exactly what
was going on, but he sensed these demons needed their
help.

Smokey slammed into the ground with enough force to
make it tremble. The hellhound rose, shook his heads, and
leapt on the giant helllizard who'd cast him aside with a
sweep of his powerful tail, savage growls ripping from his
throats while his claws and fangs tore open the creature's
scaly hide.

Sebastian cast a lightning ball at a helltigress
attempting to maul an overturned cart, behind which hid a
group of demons holding infants. He ensnared her left
hindleg with his whip as she staggered to the side and

tugged viciously. The monster snarled in fury as she was dragged through dirt and rock. Her shrieks faded when Sebastian drove the pale sword Artemus had made for him through her skull.

He yanked the weapon out and studied it with a frown. "This is a good blade."

"A thank you would have sufficed," Artemus said drily.

He had just fended off another attack when he spotted a huge demon carving a path across the battleground toward him, war axes dripping with black blood. Artemus frowned, dug his heels into the ground, and was preparing to defend his position and the fiends he was protecting when the demon spoke.

"Are you the brother of Samyaza's son?"

Artemus blinked before exchanging a startled glance with Callie and Sebastian. "Yes!"

"Come with me. We need your help!"

The demon turned and headed rapidly back the way he'd come.

"We?" Artemus hesitated before starting after him. "Who's we? And where's Drake?!"

"My lord and the goddess require your assistance. Your brother is safe. Arakiel and Vannog guard him as we speak." The demon dipped his head at Artemus over his shoulder. "I am Us'gorith. It is an honor to meet you, son of Michael."

"Sebastian and I can take care of these demons!" Callie indicated the enemy fiends around them, her eyes flashing jade. "You and Smokey go with him!"

Us'gorith batted demons and hellbeasts out of his way as he retraced his steps, Artemus and Smokey helping him clear a path. They skirted a bend in the gorge and came out on the edge of a vast plain stretching across the floor of a valley ringed by forested mountains.

Artemus's gaze skimmed the bone castle at the far end and the city at its foot before focusing on the bloodied battlefield taking up half the landscape, his heart in his throat.

War cries echoed across the prairie and the smell of death thickened the air as demons and hellbeasts fought one another in a brutal conflict that neither side was winning. Though the smaller army defending the city was outnumbered by the one who'd surrounded them, they had strong warriors in the form of several powerful demons with crimson gazes.

Artemus's pulse skittered when he saw a face he'd never thought he would see again in this lifetime amongst them. "As—*Astarte?!*"

The goddess stabbed a hellbeast in the eye with her spear and scowled at him over her shoulder from where she defended her position some eighty feet from them.

"Will you stop gaping like a moron and get your sorry ass over here?!"

"But—but how?" Artemus mumbled at Us'gorith. "I thought Otis had put her to sleep!"

"From what my lord Armaros told me, the Seal of Astaroth brought the goddess back to Hell," the demon replied as they made their way across the battlefield, Smokey carving a path for them with bloodthirsty enthusiasm. "She has been protecting your brother since he arrived in the Underworld." Us'gorith glanced at him. "It is thanks to her that he never fell into Satanael's grasp."

CHAPTER TWENTY-EIGHT

S<small>HOCK REVERBERATED THROUGH</small> A<small>RTEMUS AT THIS NEWS.</small>
He felt Smokey's surprise across their bond.

Astarte has been protecting Drake all this time?!

The ground shook violently beneath his feet. His eyes
widened at the sight of the tusked mammoth coming at
them from the right and the demon atop the beast.

Savage snarls ripped the air. Smokey bounded over and
knocked him and Us'gorith out of the path of the hellbeast's charge. His paws raked the dirt as he whirled
around to face the enemy.

Artemus glared at the crimson-eyed fiend sneering
down at them as he and Us'gorith climbed to their feet.
"Oriens!"

"We meet again, son of Michael," the demon prince
said coldly. "Satanael will be most pleased when I bring him
your head."

Fire bloomed on Artemus's blades as he called upon the
divine powers scorching his soul.

He shot up into the air and glowered at Oriens. "I

believe your master needs me alive to open the seventh gate, dumbass!"

Artemus darted under the hellmammoth's tusk and stabbed him in the right eye. The monster screamed and reared up on his hindlegs, his enormous trunk swinging to bat at Artemus. Smokey leapt onto the beast's right foreleg and took a chunk out of his tendons. Inky blood splattered across the ground as the hellmammoth keened in pain and stumbled heavily onto a knee.

"Get up!" Oriens kicked the wounded creature viciously in the flanks with his spiked boots. *"Get up, you foolish—!"*

His shout became a grunt, Artemus smashing him clear off the beast's back and into the air. The demon prince braced his wings to halt his sudden flight. He moved, figure blurring and broadsword gleaming in his grip as he let out an ungodly yell.

His blade clanged against the wing Artemus raised to protect himself. The demon froze, scarlet pupils widening.

Artemus flashed a savage smile at him. "In case you're wondering, it's made of metal and nanorobots."

He dropped, came up behind the fiend, and slashed his back with his swords. Oriens screamed, blood dripping from his damaged pinions as he sagged several feet.

"That's right, shit for brains." Artemus shouldered his weapons and grinned at the retreating demon prince. "You're looking at the first bionic angel in existence."

"Oh, *please,*" Astarte said with a disgusted air where she fought a group of fiends.

"Michael's son is as big of an idiot as he is," a demon atop a helltiger said to another demon with curved horns tipped with hellfire.

The horned demon rolled his eyes.

"Excuse Chazaquiel," he apologized to Artemus. "I'm Armaros, the—"

"Eleventh Leader of the Grigori. I know who you are. And you must be—"

Artemus paused and studied the demon on the helltiger blankly.

"I am the Eighth Leader!" Chazaquiel snapped.

"Right. Sorry."

"Zakiel, Ramiel!" Astarte bellowed at two demons fighting hordes of winged fiends in the sky. "Tamiel needs a hand!"

The Sixth and Fifteenth Leaders of the Grigori gazed to the left of the battlefield at the demon on a helllionness fending off an enormous fiend wearing armor of stone and his troops.

"On it!" Zakiel called, tucking his wings and diving while Ramiel finished off the creatures in their path.

Fire bloomed in the center of the valley. Two giant, red, horned helldragons circled one another, angry hisses and roars erupting from their jaws along with violent jets of flame. The smaller one sported several wounds on her flanks and had her tail wrapped protectively around a purple, baby helldragon huddling against her left hindleg.

Smokey let out a growl of fury, acid drool dripping heavily from his jowls. He bolted toward the warring helldragons, his powerful strides closing the distance in seconds as he bounded over and around the enemy demons and hellbeasts in his path. He landed some fifty feet from the helldragons, crouched, and sprung.

The enemy dragon shrieked as Smokey landed on his left flank and sank all his claws and three jaws full of teeth into his flesh. He snorted out a fireball and swatted at the hellhound with his barbed tail.

The female helldragon whirled around and blocked the attack with her own tail. She inhaled deeply before roaring out a jet of white-hot flames in her attacker's face, her crimson gaze blazing with fury.

Artemus's eyes widened. "*Watch out!*"

He flashed toward the beasts locked in the deadly fight, knowing he would be too late to stop the smirking, horned dragon from squashing the now exposed baby hellbeast with his forelegs.

The female dragon's nostrils flared in horror. Smokey detached himself from the larger dragon's flank, leapt over the beasts' entwined tails, and landed in front of the baby helldragon. He turned and snarled in defiance as the enemy's massive claws dropped toward him, his eyes flaring gold and the shadows engulfing him dwarfing his body.

Fear twisted through Artemus's chest. "*Smokey!*"

The air trembled high above the valley. A black hole exploded into existence several hundred feet above the hellbeasts. A demon with crimson eyes and a giant hell-dragon the color of midnight dropped out of it.

"*Get away from my son, you sack of excrement!*" the beast roared.

He slammed into the enemy dragon, raked his flank with his claws, and impaled his back with his barbed tail. The red helldragon screeched and staggered away, dark blood oozing thickly from his wounds. He rounded on the black helldragon with a growl of rage and was preparing to charge when a group of helltigers surrounded him and drove him deeper into the plains.

The black dragon headed over to the red female and

butted her gently with his head. "I'm sorry I'm late, dearest."

"It is quite alright," she purred. "You had an important mission to take care of." She sought their son with her gaze, anxious clicks sounding at the back of her throat. "Vozgan?"

The baby helldragon peeked out from behind Smokey. "I'm here, Mama."

"You saved my child." The female helldragon lowered her head and blew faint smoke over Smokey, her expression grateful. "Thank you."

Smokey huffed and tentatively licked her snout.

"Cerberus?" The black helldragon came closer. "Is that you, old friend?"

Smokey tilted his heads curiously. *I...know you. You are... Vannog.* He eyed the female helldragon. *And you are...Isaya?*

She dipped her head. "Yes."

Artemus's heart thundered against his ribs where he hovered above the prairie, his unblinking gaze locked on the black helldragon. He could sense his brother's energy coming from the beast.

"Drake? Did you—" he paused and gulped, "—did you turn into a dragon?!"

"Wow," Chazaquiel muttered. "He's even dumber than his father."

Vannog huffed out some smoke. "I am not your brother."

He carefully lifted a wing. Artemus's mouth went dry.

Drake straightened where he'd been hiding beneath the helldragon's pinion. "Did you know there was a hellowl nesting under here?"

"Oh." Vannog blinked. "Is that what that itching was?"

Drake scowled. "Itching, my ass. She and her babies tried to *eat* me!"

Smokey whined softly. He changed into his rabbit form, scampered across the ground, and scaled Vannog's foreleg and flank in a flash. Rumbles of pleasure erupted from his throat as he leapt into Drake's arms and headbutted his chest.

"Hello, pooch." Drake buried his face in the rabbit's fur and closed his eyes briefly, a look of intense relief dawning on his face. "I missed you too." A shaky smile curved his mouth when he finally met Artemus's gaze. "Hey."

He gasped as Artemus shot toward him and carried him clean off the helldragon, his arms locked solidly around Drake's body.

"Don't just 'Hey' me, you ass!" Artemus mumbled hoarsely.

Drake hugged him back just as tightly. "Sorry."

Artemus shuddered at the feel of his brother's warmth and heartbeat once more, their bond burning brightly in his soul.

I'm never letting him out of my sight again!

Drake touched Artemus's artificial pinion hesitantly, his face full of wonder. "Your wing."

Artemus drew back slightly and smiled. "Do you like it?"

Drake's eyes widened. "I can—I can feel Serena's energy in it!"

"I used her and Nate's nanorobots to make it."

Sorrow darkened Drake's gaze. "I'm sorry. I—"

"It's okay. It was meant to be." Artemus grinned. "Besides, I'm the only one with a wing like this. I'm gonna call myself the—"

"If you say bionic angel again, I will kick your ass," Astarte ground out.

Drake arched an eyebrow. "You called yourself bionic angel?"

"It's a good handle," Artemus protested.

The demon who'd accompanied Vannog out of the black hole scowled at Artemus from where he floated a short distance away. "Can I punch him?"

"You just met him, Arakiel," Armaros muttered.

The demon's eyes gleamed fervently as he stared at the pale sword in Artemus's left hand.

"He's the spitting image of his father," Ramiel said to Tamiel and Zakiel as they headed over.

"That's not necessarily a good thing," Zakiel observed drily.

The air ripped in the distance. A crimson rift formed near the forested mountain to the left of the city.

Artemus dropped to the valley floor with Drake. Smokey squirmed his way out of their hold and jumped to the ground.

Astarte joined them. "They are retreating."

They frowned at the army of enemy fiends and hell-beasts limping, flying, and scurrying into the hellish portal.

"For now," Tamiel said guardedly. "Oriens is sure to tell Satanael what happened here today. We must make haste and leave."

"Artemus!" someone shouted.

Artemus turned.

Sebastian and Callie were rushing toward them from the gorge, hordes of exhausted demon families and hell-beasts at their backs.

The Sphinx reached them first, his eyes bright with power. "Drake."

He dropped to the ground, stormed over, and hugged the dark angel.

Drake rocked back on his feet, his expression somewhat stunned. He hesitated before returning Sebastian's embrace.

Artemus beamed.

Sebastian released Drake and scowled. "That was a foolish thing to do. What if Satanael had gotten his hands on you?!"

"It's nice to see you too," Drake said wryly.

Arakiel smirked at Zakiel. "Your ex-girlfriend is here."

His crimson gaze swung from the demon to Callie.

She slowed as she joined them, a puzzled frown wrinkling her brow. "Ex-girlfriend?"

"Chimera." Zakiel's scarlet eyes flared. "You look... different. Good different."

Callie scratched her cheek lightly. "Mmm, do I know you?"

"Her divine beast and Zakiel used to be an item, way back," Astarte murmured out the corner of her mouth at the sight of Artemus and Drake's startled looks. "The Heavens were awash with gossip of their love affair."

"You mean the lurid tales of how they used to make out like hellbunnies—*ouch!*" Arakiel glowered at Tamiel and rubbed the spot on the back of his head where the demon had hit him.

Sebastian narrowed his eyes at his sister. "I see that part of her personality has not changed one bit."

"Hey!" Callie protested. She pointed an accusing finger at Zakiel. "I've never even met this guy!"

"Is that kelp in her hair?" Drake asked Artemus.

Artemus grimaced. "We kinda made a detour via a lake when we got here."

A chomping sound made them turn around.

Isaya blew out a sigh. "Vozgan, stop trying to eat the hellhound. He just saved your life."

The baby dragon looked up guiltily from where he was gently gumming on a resigned Smokey's floppy, right ear.

CHAPTER TWENTY-NINE

HARUKI SHIVERED AND RUBBED HIS GLOVED HANDS briskly where he sat in front of a fire. "As Callie would say, it's cold enough to freeze the balls off a brass monkey."

"I hear you, bro," Tom muttered.

Serena narrowed her eyes at the super soldier. "Your nanorobots can control your core temperature." She looked at Haruki. "And you're a goddamn dragon."

"Hey, I'm just trying to break the ice."

Haruki glanced at the Immortal opposite him.

Greer sighed. "Kid, I'm five hundred years old. I've survived decades of awkward silences."

"You look good for your age," Daniel murmured.

"Thanks."

Serena looked out over the makeshift campsite spread out around them.

It had been two days since they'd arrived at the ice dome in Greenland. Lou, Tom, and the super soldiers joining their fight had already set up base camp by the time Nate and the Guardians had flown in from

Chicago. She'd arrived the morning of the second day, having taken a detour to her old home outside Dresden to visit her father and make two requests. Leah had similarly stayed back in Chicago to speak with her grandmother.

Though Vlašic had grudgingly agreed to Serena's first demand to allow Greer and his team of Immortals to assist them, he had balked at the second.

"I won't ask them to do that," her father had said, his face set in stubborn lines.

"They must have foreseen this," Serena had argued. "The Immortal with the power of the Seer and the children who saved us in Greenland. They *must* have predicted this turn of events." She'd paused and swallowed. "Artemus and Drake are strong. So are the other Guardians. But there is still a chance we might lose this battle. And if that happens, it's game over for the rest of the world. So, you have to—"

Vlašic had taken her in his arms and pressed a kiss to her forehead.

"Do you really think I could ask the Immortals who rule over our race to destroy that dome while all of you are inside it?" he'd said, his voice trembling slightly. "They would refuse anyway."

"Then they are fools!" Serena had said bitterly against his chest.

"No," Vlašic had murmured. He'd pulled back and gazed steadily into Serena's eyes. "They just trust their future allies."

Serena was mulling over the words he'd told her yesterday when motion near the entrance of the ice vault drew her attention. Haruki rose, his face brightening at the sight of the figure leading the colorfully attired group who'd just arrived.

Leah looked around curiously as she closed the distance to them, her companions trailing in her wake with guarded expressions. "This place is freaky."

Haruki hugged her and greeted the men and women behind her with an easy smile. "Hey. It's nice to see you guys again."

Floyd Nolan petted the parrot on his shoulder and dipped his chin. "Haruki."

Carmen Nolan grinned and hugged her shivering iguana. "It's great to see you too."

Esther Nolan bobbed her head in agreement, her ginger cat lodged firmly under one arm.

"Who's the kid?" Tom asked Serena, eyeing the teenage witch with purple hair and a white rabbit.

Violet Nolan cut her eyes to the super soldier. "Who's the old guy?"

"Touché," Greer murmured.

The Immortal startled as a boa constrictor slithered between his boots and coiled herself near the fire.

Miles Nolan grimaced. "I'm sorry. Millie is feeling the cold."

Carmen's iguana joined the serpent.

Haruki observed the strangers who'd stopped a polite distance away. "Your grandmother agreed to send reinforcements?"

Leah grinned. "And then some." She turned and made introductions. "This is Bryony Cross, the High Priestess of the New York Coven." She indicated a woman in her fifties with ash-white hair and shrewd, gray eyes. "April Blackwood, High Priestess of the Philadelphia Coven." The elderly woman with rich, red hair and blue eyes dipped her chin regally. "And last but not least, Regina Nox, High Priestess of the Las Vegas Coven."

Nox greeted them with a jovial grin, her brown eyes sparkling under a riot of gray-speckled, curly hair. "Howdy."

Blackwood sighed. "Really, Regina?"

Cross rolled her eyes. "Howdy? Is that the best line you could come up with?"

"Hey, it beats, 'Nice to meet you and let's hope we don't all die in this fight,'" Nox said with a shrug.

The witches and sorcerers behind the High Priestesses murmured uneasily amongst themselves.

"Mother, please." A young sorcerer with a long-suffering expression and a rottweiler sitting alertly by his legs sighed at Nox. "We had a talk about this."

Nox squinted. "What, you mean about me being more tactful with my language? I'm sorry, I can't recall the exact details of that conversation right now."

"You just repeated the salient points," Cross said scathingly. She turned to Nox's son. "How about you join my coven, Erik? We could do with a talented sorcerer like you in our ranks."

Nox yanked Erik closer. "Hey, stop trying to steal my kid, you wench!"

"Here we go again," Blackwood muttered as the two High Priestesses started arguing with one another.

Serena glanced at the crowd of witches and sorcerers. "And Barbara?"

"She and Armand Duprey are advising our High Council how best to proceed," Blackwood replied briskly.

"Proceed with what?" Haruki said, puzzled.

"The End of the World," the High Priestess said somberly. "In case we fail." She frowned. "Barbara had better consider our favors paid if we survive this."

The other two High Priestesses paused long enough to nod in agreement.

"They owe your grandmother?" Haruki murmured to Leah.

"Yeah. Apparently, she saved their lives a long time ago." Leah looked around. "Where are Jacob and Otis?"

"They went to the crater with Nate to see if they could pick up a signal on Gideon's device," Serena said.

Someone shouted Leah's name in the distance. They turned.

Jacob was running toward them, his cheeks red with the cold and his eyes sparkling.

Serena thought back to the solemn child they'd met several weeks ago, when Solomon had first turned up on their doorstep. Her heart grew heavy with sorrow.

Jacob's transformation would have pleased him.

"Anything?" she called out to the men lagging behind the young Guardian.

Otis shook his head, his expression uneasy. "No."

"Not even a beep," Nate murmured.

"It's been two days," Daniel said. "Heaven only knows what kind of trouble they've ended up in down there."

CHAPTER THIRTY

ARMAROS SPAT OUT HIS MEAD AND ROARED WITH laughter, the sound attracting the stares of several demons nearby.

Zakiel grinned. "The seraph kicked Leviathan's ass?"

Artemus smirked and made a punching gesture. "Smashed him straight into a bridge and dragged him down into a rift in the river."

"Wait," Drake said. "You guys destroyed a bridge?!"

Callie grimaced. "It was two bridges actually. And half of Downtown."

"I would have liked to have seen that," Armaros wheezed, wiping tears of merriment from his eyes. "It was high time someone taught that stupid sea serpent a lesson!"

"I cannot believe Satanael sent those four to Chicago to capture you and the hellhound," Ramiel said anxiously.

"I can," Arakiel muttered.

Chazaquiel nodded.

Drake grimaced. "*I* can't believe the U.N. Special Security Council decided to imprison you and Smokey."

Artemus shrugged. "To be fair, I kinda see their logic. They just hadn't grasped how utterly powerless they would be in the face of Hell's army."

"That's not what you said when we were in Chicago," Callie observed.

"A man can change his mind," Artemus protested. He paused and looked into his drink, a thoughtful frown wrinkling his brow. "It was the strangest thing. The demon princes were scared of Otis. All of them. Leviathan was the only one who dared challenge him directly."

The demon lords glanced at one another.

"Well, if you had seen what we saw during the war that landed us here, so would you be," Tamiel said solemnly. "Besides, those two have ancient history."

Artemus and Callie stared at him, puzzled.

"Just as the seraph was God's trusted Right Hand, Leviathan bore the title of His Left Hand, before he fell," Tamiel explained. "I don't think the seraph ever forgave Leviathan his betrayal. And neither has Leviathan forgotten what Heaven's army did to him and the Grigori."

Us'gorith appeared with a queue of demons bearing giant plates of food. Smokey opened a lazy eye where he'd been snoozing on Vozgan's back. He perked up at the smell of the cooked meats the demons were laying out.

"Try the hellboar," Drake told a dubious Artemus and Callie.

Artemus hesitated before picking up a rib dripping with juices. He took a bite. Surprise shot through him.

"It's delicious," he mumbled as he chewed and swallowed. "What kind of spices are in this?"

"Demon piss and the excrement of a helldragon," Arakiel said nastily.

Artemus choked. Smokey froze where he'd started devouring an entire hellboar next to Vozgan.

Armaros slapped Artemus on the back with enough force to bring his food back up and rolled his eyes at the grinning demon across the fire. "Do not believe him. We do not use demon piss or dragon excrement in our food."

"We reserve that kind of thing for our crops," Chazaquiel said before gulping down a stewed helllizard.

Artemus took a swig of his mead and wiped his mouth. "You have crops down here?"

"We have water and earth with living creatures in them." Zakiel shrugged. "Which is more than we expected when we first arrived here."

"I have to say, the forests and the lakes were a surprise." Callie studied the camp that extended as far as the eye could see. "So were the children and your cities." She straightened. "Oh. There they are."

Astarte and Sebastian were making their way toward them through the mass of demons and hellbeasts occupying the cavern where they had sought refuge. Following the battle in Armaros's realm, they had followed Tamiel's advice to relocate their forces somewhere Satanael and Hell's Council would not easily find them. Since using a Hell portal might have alerted their enemy to their activities, they'd utilized Arakiel's ability to create black holes and Sebastian's rifts to evacuate everyone on the plains and in the city to their current location in Hell Deep.

"Did you find anything?" Tamiel asked Astarte.

She dropped down beside Drake. "No. Satanael should have started moving his forces by now." The goddess frowned. "It's too quiet. I don't like it." She paused when

Drake handed her the drink he'd poured for her. "Thank you."

Artemus glanced curiously between his twin and the goddess. "You two are awfully friendly."

Astarte arched an eyebrow. "Is that jealousy I hear in your voice?"

"No," Artemus denied. "I was just thinking of a particular super soldier who might get annoyed if she saw—" he gestured at them vaguely with a hand, "this."

Drake sighed.

Astarte grimaced. "Oh, *please*. If I had wanted to ravish your brother, I would have done so by now. Besides, I prefer cute, innocent types, like you." She grinned, exposing her fangs. "There's nothing more satisfying than defiling a pure soul."

Smokey's eyes rounded. Artemus felt the blood drain from his face.

Astarte chortled. "I'm joking. Besides, I'm sure your husband will get mad if I lay a talon on you."

"He's married?" Arakiel said in a tone of disbelief.

"The Dragon's father gave his son to him," Astarte explained. "From what Drake has said, it appears they have yet to consummate their marriage."

Artemus cut his eyes to his brother.

Drake shrugged. "It's true."

"Are you impotent?" Arakiel asked, a hopeful undertone lacing his question.

"No, I am not impotent!" Artemus snapped. "Haruki and I are *not* married, nor will we be consummating *anything*, thank you *ever* so much!"

"Poor Haruki," Callie murmured.

~

SATANAEL DRUMMED HIS CLAWS LAZILY ON THE ARMREST of his chair and observed the two demons crouched on their knees at the bottom of his throne.

"So, what you're basically saying is you failed."

Though he spoke in a low, measured tone, his voice sent an icy chill down Oriens's spine.

"Please give us another chance, my liege," the demon prince said, his dark heart thundering in his chest while his gaze remained focused on a spot below Satanael's feet. He could feel Turiel trembling beside him. "We promise not to disappoint you."

"Oh, you would never disappoint me," Satanael murmured. "But alas, every mistake has consequences."

The head of Hell's Council glanced at his most loyal subordinate.

Belial dipped his chin before signaling to the guards standing by the doors. Oriens and Turiel stiffened as two female demons were dragged kicking and screaming into the throne room by their skulls.

"I believe these two ladies have been your consorts for the last few hundred years," Satanael drawled.

Oriens swallowed and closed his eyes briefly, his black wings sagging as he listened to his lover's desperate pleas for mercy. Turiel fisted his hands and gnashed his fangs.

Satanael waved a lazy hand at Belial.

Ba'al's leader raised his broadsword and cut off the heads of the two female demons with a single swing of his blade, a savage grin distorting his monstrous face.

The fiends' bodies thudded to the ground.

Oriens's lover's bloodied skull thunked wetly against his knee, her face frozen in a mask of horror.

"Ah." Satanael brought a hand to his mouth, an expression of mock surprise on his face. "I'm sorry. I did not know they were with child."

Turiel made a pained sound.

Oriens clenched his jaw. *Like hell you didn't!*

He couldn't stop himself from glaring at his king for a fleeting second. Satanael's crimson pupils flared. Oriens lowered his gaze hastily.

Shit!

Rage bubbled in his veins as he reflected on his and Turiel's recent defeat. The face of Michael's son danced across his inner vision.

It's all that damn angel's fault!

"Belial, be so kind as to cut off Turiel's left hand," Satanael said in a bored voice. "And take one of Oriens's eyes." An expression of pure madness distorted the demon king's features for a moment. The air trembled, his wrath pulsing briefly from his enormous body and making the hall of bones tremble. "They dared to defy me, after all."

A protest fell from Turiel's jaws. Oriens silently resigned himself to his grim fate.

"Summon the rest of the council after you are done," Satanael added as Belial headed over to the two demons to perform the wicked deeds. "We have work to do."

CHAPTER THIRTY-ONE

"WE SHOULD GO TO THE SEVENTH GATE," ARTEMUS SAID stubbornly.

Astarte frowned. "We need a better plan of action than that. Besides, we don't know where the gate is."

Artemus blew out an exasperated sigh. "Like I told you, it's in Greenland."

Drake grimaced. "Anyone else still think that's a weird location for the Apocalypse?"

"I do," Callie said.

Smokey huffed in agreement.

Astarte glared at Artemus and indicated the cavern with a wave of her hand. "Do you see signs to Greenland anywhere?!"

"Then how the heck did you guys always know where to go on Earth?!"

"We were usually guided by demon lust or one of Belial's cronies."

"Besides, even if we knew the exact route to Greenland from Hell Deep, Satanael has distorted the interdimensional barriers between our worlds," Armaros added. "It means we'll be traveling blind."

"We should make sure our denizens are safe first." Tamiel gazed out broodingly over the campsite. "Not all will be joining us in our fight."

"I agree," Zakiel said.

A disturbance in the air above the cavern made them reach for their weapons. They relaxed when Sebastian and Arakiel came out of a rift.

"Our ancient bolt holes are still untouched." Arakiel dropped down beside them. "There is enough food and water in those valleys to support our people for a long time."

Ramiel brightened. "That is good news, indeed."

Artemus rubbed the back of his neck, the thought that had been preoccupying him at the forefront of his mind once more. "There's something I've been meaning to ask you guys. What happens if we do manage to leave here through the seventh gate?" He hesitated as he observed the demons, his expression awkward. "Will Satanael and Hell's Council come after you?"

Zakiel arched an eyebrow. "Are you worried about us, kid?"

Artemus flushed slightly. "What's wrong with being worried about my friends?"

Zakiel blinked in surprise. Tamiel and Ramiel smiled faintly.

Arakiel turned and made retching noises. Chazaquiel rolled his eyes at the demon.

"Hell is more than big enough for us to stay out of his way for an eternity," Astarte said. "Besides, I suspect Satanael will spend the next few hundred years trying to win us back over to his side. He knows how powerful we are." The goddess laid a hand on Artemus's shoulder, her expression solemn. "But thank you for your concern, son of Michael. If we had time, I would definitely ravish you."

"Stop that!" Artemus snapped.

Armaros turned and signaled Us'gorith over. "Tell everyone to pack up. We'll be moving soon."

The demon nodded and disappeared. A low babble soon rose around the cavern as news of their imminent departure spread across the camp.

Arakiel exchanged a glance with Sebastian. "There's something else." He frowned. "Something this guy picked up during our travels."

Astarte arched an eyebrow, her gaze swinging between the demon and the Guardian. "What is it?"

"I think I detected a signal when we were traveling through one of my rifts," Sebastian said. "It was only for a second and it was weak, but I am pretty certain it was from the device Gideon gave Serena."

Artemus's pulse accelerated. "Do you think you'll be able to find the place again?"

Sebastian nodded gravely. "Yes. It might take some time though."

"Then the sooner we start, the better."

It took the rest of the day to relocate the demons and hellbeasts faithful to Astarte and the six Grigori leaders to the places Arakiel had deemed safe from the reach of Satanael and Hell's Council. Sebastian, Artemus, and Astarte spent that time traveling to the various caverns he and Arakiel had visited that morning to try and pick up the signal from Serena's device.

It was late by the time Sebastian finally detected it

again. He stopped abruptly where they were flying through an uninhabited cavern far above Hell Deep, his gaze on the device tucked inside his pocket watch. Artemus and Astarte backtracked and joined him.

"We are close." Sebastian studied the ceiling of the cave with a frown. "I reckon the seventh gate is a few miles that way."

"Artemus, are you alright?" Concern clouded Astarte's face. "You've gone quite pale."

Artemus's head throbbed. Sweat had broken out on his forehead and his blood thundered violently in his veins.

"I feel weird." He clutched his belly and swallowed down a wave of bile. "Like I've eaten something bad."

"Then, we are definitely close," Sebastian said firmly. "Your body is reacting to the presence of your gate." He indicated the ceiling impatiently. "Shall we confirm its location? I can see an opening up there we can fit through."

Artemus grabbed his arm as he started to rise. "Wait! There's something else." He took a shaky breath, closed his eyes, and concentrated on the subtle feeling of wrongness he'd just sensed. He snapped his lids open a second later. "Can you feel that?!"

Astarte stiffened. "Yes." A muscle jumped in her jawline. "Someone is trying to mask it, but you can pick it up if you focus hard enough."

Sebastian fisted his hands. "Is that—?"

"It's Hell's armies," Astarte confirmed grimly. "They are already at the gate."

A FAINT BEEP REACHED SERENA'S EARS. HAD IT NOT BEEN for her keen hearing, she would have missed it entirely. She stilled where she sat on the edge of the crater, hands tucked in the pockets of her bomber jacket.

"Serena?"

Daniel's eyes were dark with tension where he stood beside her. He'd obviously heard the sound too.

Her pulse raced as she took out the geolocation disc. It was blinking faintly.

"Oh hell," Lou mumbled.

Serena rose and tapped her smartband, tension roiling through her. Nate answered her call on the second ring.

"Get everyone ready," she ordered curtly. "We just picked up—"

The ground shook violently beneath her feet. Ice cracked with a sound like thunder. Had Lou not grabbed her arm and yanked her toward him, she would have tumbled down the incline and into the abyss at the bottom.

Serena looked up in alarm.

The whole dome was shuddering around them.

"Daniel? What's going on?!"

Daniel froze. His eyes flashed gold. "They are coming."

A warm breeze erupted as he transformed into the Phoenix, the heavenly flames enveloping his body and giant wings dancing harmlessly over her and Lou, and casting an orange light on the ice.

"Who is—?" Lou started.

The pressure around them dropped so suddenly and so profoundly Serena felt sick.

Lou paled. "Shit!" He reached for his weapons and

glanced wildly at her. "But the gate's not open yet! Why are demons coming here?!"

Serena activated her liquid-armor suit and unsheathed the sword and knife Artemus had made for her, blood pounding in her veins. The divine power she had inherited from the Guardians rippled through her just as scores of crimson rifts tore the air above the crater. She glared at the army of demons and hellbeasts pouring out of the portals.

"Because they want to make sure Artemus and the others don't escape from Hell!"

Daniel climbed, his expression fierce. Fire bloomed in the sky as he used the Flame of God to create a barrier between them and their enemy.

CHAPTER THIRTY-TWO

ARTEMUS FOUGHT BACK THE NAUSEA TWISTING HIS GUT as he prepared to exit the black hole with Arakiel, Smokey, Armaros, and Astarte.

Shit. Is this how every Guardian feels when they're close to their gate?!

The corrupt pressure he'd sensed from inside Arakiel's portal doubled in intensity when they emerged at the end of an immense cavern. Artemus's ears popped and his skin prickled as he breathed in pure evil.

Thump.

A soft gasp left him, a fresh and inherently malevolent force pressing against his flesh. His stomach lurched.

The dark energy plucked at his body and mind through the divine armor that shielded him, an insidious compulsion that invited depravity and mindless violence.

I think I'm gonna throw up!

Smokey whined beside him, the bond that linked them trembling with unease. Artemus swallowed convulsively and followed the hellhound's unblinking gazes to the artifact calling to them.

Thump-thump.

The seventh gate loomed in the far distance, its imposing, stone doors rising some two hundred feet tall and topped by the head of a ferocious hellbeast. The light the creature emitted from his crimson pupils reflected off the bright walls around them, multiplying the unholy radiance a hundredfold until a red haze pulsed through the very air.

Armaros observed the diamond cave with an awed expression. "I had heard rumors of this place, but I never thought I would see it before the End of Days."

Astarte gripped her viper-wreathed spear tightly and stared dead ahead. "I think you should stop sightseeing and concentrate on those guys."

Amassed before the final portal of Hell was a legion of ochre-eyed demons and hellbeasts some thousand feet deep. Samyaza and Beelzebub hovered at the head of the army, along with Belial and a demon prince Artemus hadn't seen before.

The stranger was handsome in a way few fiends were, with inky wings edged with a radiance that would have been called divine were it not for the diabolic light in his vermillion eyes and the hellfire sprouting from his curved horns. Dark flames swarmed the enormous, serrated broadswords he wielded.

"*Lucifer!*" Arakiel spat.

The Morning Star flashed his fangs. "Hello, Arakiel. You look as disgustingly smug as ever."

Arakiel scowled and tightened his hold on his sword.

"You will be punished for your insolence, traitors!"

Belial roared. "Trust me, by the time I am finished with you, you will be begging for your puny lives!"

Astarte made a face. "Was he always that irritating?"

"Yeah," Armaros said glumly. "That guy's been in love with the sound of his own voice since we were in Heaven."

Artemus ignored the demons, his heart pounding and his gaze inexorably drawn to the gate once more.

Thump-thump. Thump-thump.

The portal was resonating with every fiber of his being, as if it were alive and talking to him. He knew Smokey was experiencing the same thing. After all, they'd both felt the gate summoning them while they'd been traveling through Arakiel's portal.

Artemus clenched his jaw. He knew now why the other Guardians had always looked so helpless when they'd first come face to face with their gate. It was a confrontation they could not evade. A destiny that they had to embrace. A fate that could never be denied. And it was up to each Guardian to defeat their gate if they wanted to survive the challenge.

Power surged across his bond with Smokey. He looked at the hellhound and saw the same determination throbbing through his blood fill the golden eyes opposite him.

"You with me, pooch?"

Smokey's pupils flared. *Always.*

A hateful growl erupted from the enemy frontline.

"Where is my bastard son?" Samyaza glared at Artemus. "It's about time I brought that wretch to heel!"

Artemus narrowed his eyes at the demon who had haunted his brother for as long as he had known him. "He's far away from the reach of his dirtbag father. Who, incidentally, is about to get his ass royally kicked by yours truly."

"Oh boy," Armaros muttered.

Arakiel sneered. "Trash talk? Really?"

"Hey, it worked in Chicago," Artemus protested.

Samyaza's pupils blazed with hatred.

Beelzebub tut-tutted where he floated beside the demon, his monstrous shape shrouded with thousands of flies. "You're being rude to your stepfather, little boy. We should teach you to respect your elders."

Artemus made a face. "No offense but I think my elders should have a bath first. I mean, do you even smell yourself?"

The demon prince blurred.

Artemus blocked Beelzebub's blade an inch from his head and tried not to gag as the fiend's foul miasma enveloped him. Smokey snarled.

Astarte, Armaros, and Arakiel surrounded the demon prince, their weapons pressing hard against his body. Beelzebub paid them no heed.

"I'm going to enjoy seeing you bleed, angel!" he spat in Artemus's face. "And I shall feast on your intestines while you are still breathing!"

Artemus scowled. "Has anyone ever told you demons you have an unhealthy obsession with people's guts?"

He headbutted Beelzebub in the nose, whipped the pale, glowing blade strapped to his back from its sheath, and slashed him across the chest.

The demon prince hissed as the sword carved through his armor and traced a thin cut in his flesh. He extended his wings and shot back to the enemy frontline, his crimson pupils flashing with shock and a trickle of dark blood oozing from his flesh.

The other demon princes glanced from his wound to Artemus, their faces twisting with a mixture of disquiet and fresh loathing.

"What is that weapon you wield, you infidel?!" Belial barked.

"I'm glad you asked." Artemus grinned and propped the sword on his shoulder. "I call it—"

"Please don't—" Astarte begged.

"—The Great—" Artemus continued.

"Oh dear God," Arakiel murmured in disgust. "He's given it a stupid name, hasn't he?"

"—Demon Butt Kicking Sword," Artemus finished.

He beamed at Hell's armies.

A leaden silence ensued.

"Wow," Armaros mumbled.

Astarte glared at Artemus. "I'm gonna kill you."

Smokey let out an embarrassed huff.

Arakiel grumbled something under his breath and waved a hand. The air wavered near the gate. A score of giant blackholes opened behind Hell's armies, raising startled shrieks from the mass of fiends.

"Hey!" Artemus scowled at Arakiel and pointed at the rippling portals. "I thought we were doing that later!"

"The urge to bitchslap you into Hell Deep is getting stronger, so the sooner we end this battle, the better," Arakiel snapped.

Demons and hellbeasts poured out of the black holes, Sebastian, Callie, and the Grigori leaders at their head. Vannog's enormous body exited a portal a moment later, towering over them all.

Drake sat on the helldragon's back. A frown darkened his face when he found Samyaza with his gaze.

"Hello, Father."

CHAPTER THIRTY-THREE

SERENA DUCKED BENEATH THE HELLDRAGON AND SLASHED his left hindleg. The beast roared and kicked out viciously. She jumped clear of his foot, missed his swinging tail by a hairbreadth as it arced above her chest, and somersaulted into the air. She landed on her feet and skidded backward across the ice, her stance steady and her bloodied blades firm in her grip.

Battle cries rose around the ice dome as their side engaged the vast enemy army who had appeared before them. They were holding their ground, despite being outnumbered four to one.

Serena knew it was thanks to Otis that they had not yet fallen.

Even though the third point of his second star had yet to manifest on his left palm and he did not have access to the golden broadsword he had used in Chicago to defeat Hell's troops, he was still a formidable opponent for the demon princes they currently faced.

Leviathan shrieked in rage as Otis held him and hordes

of demons and hellbeasts prisoner within a giant, divine sphere some hundred feet above the ground. Flames washed across the inner wall of the globe as the sea serpent breathed out a river of fire. The blaze caught some of the fiends and beasts inside the barrier and vaporized them into oblivion.

Daniel protected Otis's back, the Flame of God taking the form of dozens of powerful weapons as he defended the seraph against the swarm of winged demons and hell-beasts attempting to bring him down.

Motion atop the helldragon who had just attacked her drew Serena's wary gaze once more.

Ariton unsheathed his blade and scowled at her from where he sat astride his beast. "It seems I shall have to deal with you myself, little rat!"

The demon prince rose from his ride, his dark wings stark against the pale vault above them and his crown and eyes pulsing with an evil light. Smoke puffed from his hell-dragon's nostrils as he turned to face her, his glare as wicked as his master's.

Nate appeared on her left, his armor and skin aglow with divine radiance. "Need a hand?"

Lou materialized on her right, Tom at his side. "How about two more?"

A grim smile formed on Serena's lips as she glanced at her friends. "This kinda feels like old times."

Tom scratched his cheek with the handle of his blade. "Hmm, I hate to bring this up, but we never fought demons in the old times."

Lou frowned. "You're ruining the moment."

Serena swore as they were dragged several feet across the ice toward Ariton's dragon. The hellbeast was taking a giant breath, his chest and neck swelling to gargantuan proportions as he sucked in all the air in the vicinity.

"Uh-oh," Tom mumbled.

Ariton dove, his broadsword carving through the air with a hiss.

Serena deflected the blade a foot from her heart. The ice gave beneath her as the demon pushed at her with all his might. Nate slammed into his left flank with a roar.

An orange glow lit the helldragon's jaws.

"Fire in the hole!" Lou yelled.

Heat scorched Serena's left thigh. The liquid-armor suit reacted automatically, its power strengthened by divine light and shielding her flesh from damage. Her eyes widened as she watched the beast's flames dance across the ice toward the three men.

"*Nate!*"

The jet of fire followed Nate as he moved, its speed and power more than matching his supernatural abilities. Serena's heart lurched. She scowled at the demon obstructing her path.

Ariton sneered. Serena glanced at Nate, panic thrumming through her.

Shit!

A large shape dashed in front of the super soldier and took the brunt of the blaze a second before it reached him. Serena's pulse quickened as she stared at the divine beast towering protectively over Nate.

"Are you okay?" Jacob growled.

Nate swallowed and nodded.

Serena shivered, the fierce light in the Guardian's eyes resonating with the energy inside her.

The Hydra's serpentine heads twisted around in unison.

Jacob glared at the dragon before turning to face him, his dark scales unmarked by the hellfire that had washed across his back and tail. He spun his staff above his heads, gripped the pale blade Artemus had made for him, and charged the monster.

Brightness blossomed inside Serena as the bond that linked her to all the Guardians flared deep within her soul and filled her with power. Nate's eyes flashed gold. He straightened and headed toward her, his skin and armor glowing, his pace picking up speed.

Serena gritted her teeth, drew on all her strength, and shoved back against Ariton as the three super soldiers converged on them.

GREER WIPED BLOOD FROM HIS MOUTH, HIS CHEST heaving with his breaths. "I believe we are in a pickle."

"No shit, Sherlock," the female super soldier beside him murmured, the wound on her flank healing with preternatural speed.

Her deadly gaze remained focused on the ring of demons and hellbeasts encircling them at the south end of the crater.

Leah's heart thudded against her breast as she observed their enemy. *There's a lot of them.*

Her beast spoke. *We are stronger.*

Leah smiled faintly. The Lion's confidence had never once faltered since she first embraced his presence.

She inhaled shakily. *Lion?*

Yes?

Thank you. For choosing me as your host.

Heat bloomed inside her. *You are worthy of my powers, child.*

Leah breathed out and breathed in. Her racing pulse slowed. Static danced across the thin, golden armor covering her body. It arced onto the tips of her claws and exploded up the length of the double-ended, three-pronged spear in her hand.

Storm clouds burst into existence high above her. The smell of ozone swelled as she drew on the blinding light within her core and the beast who had blessed her with his soul. Together, they called on the power of the fallen angel who had gifted them his divine weapon and unleashed a violent lightning storm upon their enemy.

The detonation ripped through the horde, casting fiends and monsters dozens of feet into the air. Hellish shrieks filled Leah's ears as they smashed down onto the ice, their battered bodies splattering dark blood across the pale ground.

The Immortals and super soldiers hunkered down around her slowly straightened in the aftermath of the explosion.

"Well, that was different." Greer eyed the sparks flickering on the Spear of Ramiel with a guarded expression before staring at the group of winged demons flying toward them from left field. "Think you can do that again? 'Cause here comes some more—"

"Leah, watch out!"

Leah's stomach lurched as Haruki's warning tore toward her from where he fought Oriens. She whirled around and cursed at the sight of the dark broadsword winging its way toward them at the end of a long tentacle, its serrated edges brimming with hellfire. Though she knew the gesture was futile, she started spinning her spear to try and deflect it from the Immortals and super soldiers at her side.

Gold and purple symbols flashed into existence two feet in front of her. Lines exploded from the arcane markings, forming a glowing, magic shield that stopped the sword short of impaling her left eye.

Violet dropped down beside her, her eyes alight with power. "Who's Squid Guy?"

Miles landed next to the young witch, his gaze reflecting the golden spheres of magic spinning above his palms.

Relief flared through Leah. It never ceased to surprise her how powerful her cousins were.

She glared at the demon prince who had attacked them. "His name is Maggot."

"He's one fugly SOB," Miles muttered.

Maggot sneered from atop his saber-toothed helltiger. "Your insults will not work against me, children of Azazel."

"Oh yeah?" someone said icily. "Well, maybe this will."

April Blackwood's eyes flashed a cerulean blue as she directed the magic-wreathed blades and balls of pure energy wielded by the witches and sorcerers at her side at the demon prince.

Maggot screeched in outrage, the barrage smashing into his tentacles and the hide of his hellbeast. They whirled around and glared at the witches and sorcerers.

"How do you like them pears?!" Regina Nox said gleefully.

Erik Nox sighed. "It's apples, Mother."

Bryony Cross pinched the bridge of her nose and muttered something under her breath.

CHAPTER THIRTY-FOUR

DRAKE'S KNUCKLES WHITENED WHERE HE CLUNG TO Vannog. Coldness surged inside his body, the evil that had always lived within his soul battering at the prison that held it back by the slimmest of threads. His skin prickled, as if a thousand needles were piercing his skin.

He could feel the gate at his back. Could feel it calling to him. Telling him to give in to it. Enticing him to embrace the darkness that was his inheritance.

Heat bloomed in his gut.

Drake sucked in air and stared over Hell's armies to the Guardians who stood at the other end of the cavern. The ones who had always been by his side. The ones who would *always* protect him, come what may.

Artemus and Smokey's eyes glowed brightly as they met his gaze, their expressions fierce and their bond filling his mind and body with dazzling brilliance. Warmth surged through Drake's veins and flesh once more. He shuddered.

Beneath the power that threatened to consume him, he could sense Theia's comforting strength.

"I see you have taken the side of our foe after all." Samyaza sneered at him from the enemy's frontline, his wicked gaze blazing with disdain. "It seems I shall have to show you the error of your ways, you ungrateful knave!"

Drake frowned. "Hey, Artemus?"

"Yeah?"

Drake flashed a vicious smile at Samyaza. "Make sure you kick his ass *real* hard."

Artemus smirked. "Sure thing."

Drake took a deep breath and finally let loose the power swelling inside him. Wings sprouted from his back. Dark armor exploded across his body. His knife and watch transformed into deadly weapons, the serrated broadsword bathed in hellfire. And across them all, the crimson sigils that marked him as the key to the last gate of Hell appeared, the symbols glowing vividly against an inky backdrop of metal and skin.

The air trembled, the pressure inside the cavern dropping further as the gate resonated with its key.

Drake rose from the black helldragon and headed for the giant, stone doors, the holy ties that linked him to his Guardians keeping the darkness within him at bay.

"*Stop him!*" Belial roared. "It is not yet time for the gate to open!"

Drake wondered at that odd statement as Ba'al's leader spread his enormous wings and shot toward him, Beelzebub and a horde of winged demons in his wake.

Zaqiel climbed into the path of their enemy, Tamiel, Chazaquiel, and a troop of winged hellbeasts at his side. "I don't think so."

Vannog moved protectively in front of Drake.

A thunderous din exploded across the cavern as demon clashed against demon.

~

LUCIFER GLARED AT ASTARTE OVER THEIR CROSSED weapons.

"You have fallen low, Goddess!" the Morning Star hissed. "Did the loss of Ishiem affect your reasoning?"

Astarte clenched her jaw. *"Do not take his name, you lowlife!"*

Her vipers swarmed Lucifer's swords and arms and wrapped around his neck. Lucifer grunted, muscles bunching as he tried to break free of her hold.

Something flickered out of the corner of Astarte's eye. She shot backward and narrowly avoided the dark blade that hummed past her face.

Beelzebub's flies swarmed the air as he joined Lucifer. The demon prince frowned heavily at Astarte.

"It's such a shame. You were given a much-coveted position in Hell's Council. Yet, you chose to sacrifice it all. And for what? The man you love is dead, the temples where you were once worshipped long defiled." Beelzebub extended a hand toward her, his crimson eyes bright with persuasion. "It is not too late to join us, Sister. I am certain He will forgive you for this transgression. He is our king after—"

A figure smashed into the demon prince's flank. They hurtled through the air and crashed into the wall of the cavern, a cloud of bright shards filling the air in the wake of the explosion.

Samyaza's monstrous form appeared through the

sparkling mist. He pushed away from the crater he and Beelzebub had carved into the rockface, a growl rumbling from his throat. Beelzebub coughed and scowled behind him.

"Sorry!" Artemus appeared beside Astarte. "Did I interrupt something?"

"It was nothing important," Astarte murmured.

She knew better than to be tempted by the words of her fallen brethren. She had made that mistake once before and it had cost the one she loved the most his life. She fisted her hands.

Never again will I fall for their lies.

Metal clanged violently behind her. She looked over her shoulder to where Armaros and Arakiel had blocked Lucifer's blades inches from her back.

"You always were a sneaky bastard, even when we were in Heaven," Arakiel spat at Lucifer.

"It takes one to know one, Ari," Lucifer sneered.

Artemus arched an eyebrow at Astarte. "His nickname is Ari?"

Arakiel scowled at Artemus. "Don't even *think* about calling me that!"

"You're hurting my feelings, bro."

Samyaza bellowed and came at Artemus.

The angel flitted out of his path with an "Ooops!" that only amplified the demon's rage. Beelzebub smashed into Artemus's back and drove him toward the ground.

"Hey, not fair!" Artemus protested with a fading scream.

Armaros glanced at Astarte. "You're gonna miss him when he's gone, aren't you?"

Astarte grimaced. "Like I'd miss a rash." She pursed her

lips and watched Artemus's dazzling, white form as he engaged Beelzebub and Samyaza. "I should have ravished him when I had the chance."

Armaros chuckled. Arakiel made a disgusted face.

DRAKE SHUDDERED. HE PRESSED HIS HANDS AGAINST THE doors of the seventh gate. The stone was ice cold to the touch, leeching all warmth from his fingers even through his metal gauntlets. He closed his eyes and concentrated on the arcane symbols slowly taking shape inside his soul.

"How are you doing?!" Callie yelled from where she fought a group of hellbeasts to his left.

"I'm almost there."

"Sooner would be better!" Zaqiel shouted on his right, swinging at a hellish horde from atop his horned helldragon.

Sebastian cursed behind Drake. He, Chazaquiel, and Tamiel were stopping Belial from attacking him.

"Hurry!" the Sphinx bellowed.

Vannog grunted as he pushed at the helltigers trying to shred Drake to pieces, their claws and fangs raking harmlessly against his impenetrable hide.

Drake gritted his teeth and drowned out the noise of the battle by sheer strength of will. Soon, the only sound filling his ears was the beat of his heart. It was echoed by two others, their bright cadence mimicking his own and lending him divine strength.

Golden runes flashed before Drake's inner vision. His mouth parted.

The first word fell from his lips.

The gate trembled. A line of pure blackness tore up the center of the doors.

∽

SATANAEL OPENED HIS EYES. HE SIGHED, LOWERED HIS steepled hands to the armrests of his throne, and slowly uncrossed his legs.

"What a pity," he murmured to the empty hall. "And here I thought they would be able to take care of this troublesome matter on their own."

The demon king rose and took hold of the giant, crimson broadsword leaning against the ceremonial chair. The blade scraped against bone as he descended the steps of his pedestal, his stride leisurely. He strolled toward the exit and pondered how he should punish his armies and the demon princes who made up his council.

They, more than anyone, knew that the gate could only be opened when *he* deemed it to be the right time. And today was not that day.

After losing so many demons and the Nephilim in their recent battles with the Guardians and their allies, he had but a fraction of the forces he intended to unleash upon the lowly humans he loathed. He knew that he needed a much larger army to defeat their enemies if his plans were to have any chance of success. His intention had been to entrap the Guardians of the seventh gate and their key in Hell while he readied his troops to destroy the Earth.

Stop, Satanael.

Satanael froze, the Voice reverberating inside his skull. Rage filled him, magnifying the madness that had clouded his thoughts for eons. His talons curled around the handle of his blade.

"*Get out of my head!*" he roared.

I am here for you. I have always been here, my child.

Satanael dropped his weapon and clawed at his ears until they bled.

"No! You lie! I hate you! *YOU ARE NO GOD OF MINE!*"

Sorrow filled him then, so titanic in its magnitude his breath caught in his throat. Fury replaced it the next instant. He knew it wasn't his own feelings he was experiencing in that moment, but the emotions of the being who had been with him every hour of every day since he had been cast into this dark place of despair.

The agony of the betrayal he had suffered at the hands of the one who had created him and his so-called brethren stormed through him once more. It focused into a single thought and an absolute conviction.

A frightful smile twisted Satanael's lips. He picked up his sword and headed for the exit, bloodlust filling his vision with a red haze.

"I will kill them. I will kill the Guardians and their key, gate be *damned!*"

CHAPTER THIRTY-FIVE

A SHIVER RACED DOWN ARTEMUS'S SPINE. HE PARRIED
Samyaza's blade and looked over his shoulder to the far end
of the cave. Something was coming. And he had an inkling
who it was that was headed their way. He clenched his jaw.

Looks like he's finally making his move!

Air whooshed past Artemus's head. He flicked his
wings and avoided the attack by a hairbreadth.

"You should concentrate on our fight, son of Michael!"
Samyaza snarled.

Artemus glanced past the demon to the gate. The dark
line in the center throbbed as if it were alive, its inky
tendrils crawling across pale stone and creeping onto the
armor of the dark angel who was opening it. He could
barely make out his brother's shape through the army who
sought to protect him and the demons trying to kill him.
But he could *feel* him and the wondrous energy growing
across their bond.

Artemus smiled grimly.

I was right. We were nowhere near our full powers!

Samyaza's sword blurred as he launched into a furious charge. Artemus evaded every strike he tried to land with effortless grace. Beelzebub roared and came at him from the left.

Artemus blocked both demon princes' swords with his blades.

Surprise flashed in Samyaza and Beelzebub's eyes.

~

BLOOD THUNDERED IN DRAKE'S EARS AS HE STARTED TO give voice to the last incantation. His skin quivered and his muscles trembled, the unholy force swelling within him so strong he felt it would shatter his body. The runes on his armor and skin were turning gold one by one. The metal of his sword and shield started to lighten, as did the plates covering his body and his wings.

Drake. My son.

Drake inhaled shakily as Theia's voice whispered across his mind.

It is time.

A sliver of fear bolted through him for an instant.

It is okay to be afraid, child. Just remember. You are not alone.

Drake shuddered. The final word fell from his lips.

There was a moment of breathless stillness.

He gasped as the ties linking him to Artemus and Smokey exploded through his consciousness, filling him with holy radiance.

Not just our bond. I can—I can feel the others too!

~

HARUKI BLINKED. THE SWORD OF CAMAEL WAS GROWING brighter in his grip, its flames so dazzling they almost blinded him. Oriens's good eye rounded opposite him, crimson pupil flaring.

Drake!

Haruki could sense the dark angel's energy faintly. It was resonating with his own. He shivered.

No. Not just resonating. It's amplifying my powers!

"What is going on?!" Oriens snarled, the ugly wound that was his left eye oozing dark blood.

Maggot screamed in the distance. Haruki looked over and glimpsed Leah through the hordes of demons and hell-beasts separating them. His pulse stuttered.

Her spear was glowing with the same energy engulfing his weapon and her eyes blazed with the same furious strength filling his veins as she attacked the demon prince.

Haruki took a deep breath and glared at Oriens.

Let's finish this!

DANIEL SHUDDERED, THE FIRE ENGULFING HIM SO WHITE it made the ice above him glow with an ethereal light.

The demons and beasts attacking him withdrew uneasily, as if they sensed the change within him. The change happening to *all* the Guardians.

A powerful force rocked the dome and made the air tremble. Daniel twisted around, his wings fanning wide as he hovered in place. His breath caught in his throat.

The third point of Otis's second star had appeared on his left palm.

Brightness swallowed the seraph. A golden rift opened

next to his right hand. He reached inside and withdrew his sacred weapon, his expression fierce and his grip firm.

Leviathan thrashed inside the divine sphere, his scarlet eyes full of hate as he rammed the barrier repeatedly to try and reach his nemesis.

AIR LOCKED IN ARTEMUS'S LUNGS AS THE HEAT GROWING inside his soul went supernova. Fire raced through every vein and nerve ending in his body, the power it brought so intense he feared it would scorch him from the inside out and break his bones.

A yelp of surprise escaped Beelzebub as the force emanating from Artemus pushed the demon prince back some dozen feet. Samyaza roared and tried to attack Artemus, to no avail.

Flesh shifted on Artemus's back. His damaged wing sprouted anew, scattering the artificial pinions he had made and the nanorobots holding them together to the distant ground. Symbols exploded across his golden armor.

The same symbols that now covered Drake from his head to his toes.

Artemus stared from his brother's fair hair and white wings to his bright armor and the pale, serrated broadsword now brimming with divine flames in his hand. He looked down and gazed in wonder at Smokey's new form.

Golden plates swarming with runes enveloped the hellhound from his heads down. His body had swelled once more, gaining another fifteen feet in height and almost as much in width. And there, sprouting from his enormous back, was a pair of immense, white wings.

Cerberus met Artemus's eyes. *He is coming.*

Artemus followed his gaze to a point at the back of the cavern. A black spot formed on the diamond wall even as they watched. It grew exponentially, forming a rift pulsing with wicked darkness.

A monstrous shape covered in crimson armor stepped out of the hellish portal, the hellblade in his right hand almost as big as him.

Artemus smiled grimly. "Let's go say hi."

SATANAEL BLOCKED THE HOLY SWORD SWINGING AT HIS chest with a single hand. He ignored the divine flames scorching his skin, closed his talons around the blazing blade, and smirked at the fair being floating in front of him.

"Is that all you have, son of Michael?"

The cavern trembled under the power of his voice.

The impudent smile that split the mouth of the white angel made the demon king blink.

Satanael scowled. *He looks just like his traitor of a father!*

"Nope." Artemus Steele grinned. "I just needed you to look my way, asshole."

Something huge and powerful smashed into Satanael from below and carried him toward the roof of the diamond cave. The demon king snarled, grabbed the hellhound by the scruff of his enormous neck, and cast the beast from his body before he could drive him into the rockface.

Cerberus twisted, pushed against the roof with his powerful legs, and came at him again, his golden eyes blazing.

Satanael hissed in disgust and batted the hellhound with his crimson blade, denting his armor.

The strike barely slowed Cerberus. He raked the air with his claws and wings to adjust his trajectory and climbed again, unholy growls rumbling from his throats.

"Did you forget about me?" someone said above the demon king.

Wrath filled Satanael when he looked up into the white angel's grin. He roared and raised his blade to counter the attack he knew was coming.

Artemus's eyes flashed a brilliant white. He swung his swords.

Metal clashed against metal in a dazzling explosion of sparks. Surprise darted through Satanael, his armor trembling under the impact. A shocked gasp left him, the momentum of the blow kicking in and driving him toward the cavern floor at a dizzying speed. Cerberus flashed past him and added a vicious back-kick before joining the white angel.

"Oh, I say! Well done, that hound!" Vannog bellowed.

Rock detonated around Satanael as he struck the ground.

CHAPTER THIRTY-SIX

A SHOCKED SILENCE WASHED ACROSS THE CAVERN. HELL'S armies froze, stunned by what they had just witnessed. Belial blubbered in rage.

Artemus raised a hand above his eyes and squinted at the massive hole where Satanael had disappeared.

"Did we hit him too hard?" he muttered to the hellhound floating at his side.

Cerberus blew out unrepentant huffs.

The pressure inside the cave plummeted.

Artemus's breath plumed in front of his face. "Uh-oh."

"Congratulations on pissing off the king of the Underworld, you *ass!*" Arakiel yelled at him.

"He didn't exactly come here for a chit-chat," Artemus protested.

He winged his way rapidly across the cave toward Drake, Smokey at his side.

A battery of frowns greeted them when they landed in front of the gate, chief among them his twin's, those of the two Guardians standing next to him, and that of the goddess between them.

Artemus shrugged. "What?"

"Moron," Astarte muttered.

Drake shook his head while Callie and Sebastian let out long-suffering sighs. Even Vannog rolled his eyes.

Debris erupted in the middle of the cave as Satanael rose from the depths of Hell, power pulsing off him in dark waves and filling the air with suffocating corruption. The demon king roared in fury.

The cavern shook violently. Cracks appeared in the walls and ceiling.

The stone doors of the seventh gate creaked open behind Artemus and Drake.

THE SERAPH LOOKED DOWN AT HIS LEFT PALM. THE FINAL point of his star was slowly forming on his skin. With it came a flood of ancient memories and the first taste of his ultimate power. A faint smile curved his lips.

Just like old times, huh?

The ground trembled beneath him.

The crater in the center of the dome started to cave in.

Alarmed shrieks escaped demons and hellbeasts as they tumbled into the widening void.

The seraph waved a hand and carefully levitated the Guardians and the ones aiding them out of harm's way. He dropped the divine shield holding back the former Left Hand of God and watched the beast dart toward him, eyes blazing with loathing.

Leviathan froze some hundred feet away.

The demon prince looked up. His crimson pupils flared in horror.

Gasps rose from the armies below.

The seraph slowly raised his left hand toward the sea of blazing, golden swords that had appeared in the sky above him. He ignored everything and everyone around him, his gaze and his third eye focused unblinkingly on the growing abyss below.

An expectant hush fell inside the dome.

The sound that rent the air in the seconds that followed deafened everyone but him and the divine Guardians.

THE FREEZING WIND MADE ARTEMUS'S EYES WATER AS HE ascended from the bowels of the Earth, the walls of the borehole growing narrower the higher he climbed. He grunted and moved deftly out of the way of the demons and hellbeasts falling past him in a ghastly shower of misshapen forms.

"We need to stop them!" Drake shouted beside him.

"I know!"

They twisted to a hover in mid-air and watched the army of demons rising in the distance beneath them, Satanael and Hell's Council at their head.

"You guys keep going!" Astarte yelled. "We'll hold them back!"

She tucked her wings and dove, Armaros and the other Grigori leaders dropping around her. The goddess swore colorfully when Artemus, Drake, and Smokey appeared next to them.

"What the hell are you doing?!" she roared. "*Go, dammit!*"

"We're not abandoning you!" Artemus scowled at the demons soaring toward them. "Besides, I still owe someone an ass kicking!"

"Where the heck are they?!" Callie barked.

Sebastian carried her over the rim of the crevasse and lowered her to the ice, his heart thundering against his ribs and his body still vibrating with the incredible power gifted to him by the Guardians of the seventh gate and their key.

"I do not know!"

"Callie!" someone shouted to their right.

Jacob dashed toward them, Leah and Haruki following. Daniel landed between Callie and Sebastian, his flames humming with a gentle roar as they washed over their bodies.

A muscle jumped in Sebastian's jawline. "They were right behind us."

He fisted his hands and glared at the dark void, the anxiety twisting his gut resonating across his bond with the other Guardians.

Callie gasped. Sebastian stiffened and whirled around. She was staring at the sky, her face slowly draining of blood. He followed her gaze.

His pulse stuttered as he beheld the seraph floating above them and the expanse of holy swords poised in mid-air.

Brightness exploded around Drake as he shot out of the abyss and emerged beneath a giant vault of ice, Artemus and Smokey hot on his tail. He glimpsed the divine weapons in the sky and rose rapidly to the seraph's side, his heart racing. He didn't know what was happening, but he sensed inherently that Otis was the key to ending this battle.

Artemus halted some fifty feet below them. He waited until Astarte and the Grigori leaders had cleared the crater before barking an order at Otis.

"*Now!*"

The seraph lowered his hand in a graceful motion, as if he'd been waiting for the command. The divine swords dropped with deadly speed, their aim true.

Satanael's scream of fury made the world tremble as the blades drove him and his army back toward the gate of Hell.

"*You will pay for this!*" Samyaza yelled. "We will chase you to the ends of the—"

His words ended with a grunt, Artemus diving at breakneck speed and punching him in the face. The demon smashed into the wall of the crater and tumbled into the void after his king and the rest of Hell's Council, a shocked expression distorting his bloodied features.

"I told him I would kick his ass," Artemus said defensively at Astarte's expression.

The abyss started to close, debris slowly filling it from the top down.

Drake shivered at the rumble of Hell's gate closing far below.

"We have to go!" Astarte told the Grigori leaders.

They moved toward the shrinking crevasse.

"Wait!" Artemus darted in their path. "Stay!"

Drake's heart stuttered. He joined his brother, the seraph following behind him.

Astarte and the other demons exchanged startled glances.

"We can't," Arakiel said curtly. He looked around the ice dome, a hungry expression flashing in his crimson eyes for a moment. "It is not yet time for us to return to this realm."

"He is right," the seraph murmured, his words ringing in their ears.

"That was quite a show," Tamiel told him guardedly.

The seraph smiled as he observed the goddess and the demons. "It is good to see you, my friends."

"Yeah, yeah, it's just peachy," Zaqiel grumbled, his ears reddening in embarrassment. "Come on, we have to go."

Drake felt Artemus's misgivings across their bond as they watched the demons head for the void. "We'll see them again. Besides, we can't destroy the seventh gate until the time of their redemption."

Artemus sighed. "I know." He glanced at the pale sword in his left hand. A frown wrinkled his brow. "Hey, Armaros!"

The demon lord paused and turned around. "What is it?"

Artemus waved the weapon. "Do you remember what I told you about how I made this sword?"

"Of course!" Armaros gushed. "It was most fascinating."

Artemus cast the blade at him.

Surprise widened Armaros's crimson eyes. He caught the sword by its handle.

"It's yours." Artemus smiled. "Make good use of it and

my instructions. And say goodbye to Vannog and Vozgan for us!"

Armaros grinned. "I will."

He turned and winged his way toward the Grigori leaders.

Astarte hesitated, her expression torn. "Oh, what the hell!"

She rose rapidly toward Artemus, clasped the back of his neck, and kissed him. Artemus gasped, eyes rounding and wings growing limp with shock.

Callie covered the Dragon's eyes below them. "Don't look, Haruki."

Astarte ended the kiss, licked her lips, and smiled. "Sweet. Like an unplucked flower."

Artemus spluttered, face growing bright red. The goddess laughed and dropped into the void.

"Bye, Ari!" Drake called out.

Arakiel's incensed roar rose from the depths of the Earth. "I told you assholes not to call me by that—"

The seventh gate of Hell boomed shut behind the demon and his companions.

CHAPTER THIRTY-SEVEN

Deafening silence descended inside the ice dome in the aftermath of the portal's closure. The lingering sadness in Artemus's heart weighed him down as he drifted to the ground with the others. Though he had known Astarte and the Grigori leaders for only a short time, he felt their absence keenly.

"Don't worry. Once Satanael lifts the block on Hell's rifts, they will be able to travel to this realm and visit."

Artemus stared at Otis. "How do you know that?"

His assistant was changing back into his human form, the third eye on his forehead and the stars on his palms fading.

"I—I don't know." Otis hesitated before rubbing the back of his neck, his expression awkward. "I think I sensed it in my seraph form?"

Artemus mulled this over. "I guess it isn't that strange. Although I had never seen those divine swords of yours, I had an inkling what you could do with them." He sighed.

"Astarte and the others? They are good people. Even that crabby Ari."

"I suspect Arakiel was born with a frown."

Artemus smiled at that.

"*Drake!*"

Serena shouldered her way through the crowd of men and women watching them guardedly from a distance and bolted into Drake's arms. They fell to the ground in a tangle of limbs, his laughter cut short as she took his mouth in a desperate kiss.

The happiness and love shining from his brother's soul almost blinded Artemus across their bond.

"Your hair," Serena mumbled against Drake's lips as they sat up. She touched his head dazedly before tracing his feathers with her fingers. "And your wings. How—?!"

"This is our final transformation," Drake replied with a grin. "Cool, huh?"

Serena kissed him ardently, her eyes gleaming. "Yes."

Artemus scanned the wary mass studying them.

"I see a lot of new faces," he murmured to Otis.

"Barbara convinced the witches' council to send reinforcements," Leah explained.

"Your wing." Haruki stared at Artemus. "It grew back."

Artemus beamed. "Yup." He extended his pinions. "It was the power of Drake's love for me."

"No, it wasn't," Drake protested. "And don't say it like that. You're making it sound dirty."

He climbed to his feet, a flushed Serena clasping his hand as if she never intended to let go.

"Was that Astarte?" Leah mumbled, her gaze on what was left of the crater.

"It was." Callie smiled faintly. "She saved Drake when he fell to Hell."

Serena startled. "She did?"

"Yes." Drake tightened his hold on her. "She was pretty amazing."

Serena's expression grew cool. "Pretty amazing, huh?"

"I told you she'd get jealous," Artemus said smugly.

"Hey, I'm not the one she kissed!" Drake protested.

Artemus grimaced. "Don't remind me."

"Wow." Tom walked up to Smokey and stared wide-eyed at his golden armor and white wings, several of the witches and sorcerers trailing hesitantly in his wake. "You look *awesome!*"

The hellhound huffed, lowered his giant heads, and licked him with all three tongues. The newcomers eyed the drool dripping off the super soldier and maintained a safe distance.

"I hate to break up your sickening reunion, but someone's coming this way," Violet said.

Artemus followed her gaze. A man was striding across the ice toward them from the west.

Artemus's eyes widened. "Elton?!"

Elton closed the distance to them at a rapid pace and engulfed him in a fierce hug. "Thank God!"

Artemus squeezed his arms tightly around his mentor and best friend, relief replacing surprise. Though he had been confident in his plans to rescue Drake from Hell, he'd always known there was a risk none of them would make it back. He swallowed a shaky sigh.

I'm glad we did.

"Who are they?" Sebastian said guardedly.

Callie and the other Guardians stepped to his side, their faces similarly wary.

Artemus followed their stares past Elton. A group of people was approaching in the distance. He froze, the same shock reverberating through him echoing across his bond with the others.

They could all sense the divine energy swirling around the men and women walking steadily toward them, their steps confident and their expressions relaxed.

Even from a distance, Artemus could tell how incredibly powerful each of them was in their own right. Together, they presented a formidable front. One as powerful as the army who stood behind him.

Elton let him go and turned. "They brought me here." He glanced at Artemus, his expression puzzled. "They said they knew you guys."

The world stilled around Artemus. His heart thudded painfully in his chest at the sight of the woman at the head of the party.

Her eyes were the color of a stormy sea. Her long, lustrous, chestnut hair curled gently around her face, framing her refined features and creamy skin. A dazzling smile parted her lips.

Artemus trembled, his gaze locked unblinkingly on hers.

She was even more beautiful than in his dreams.

"Artemus?" Drake said in a tone full of wonder. "Is she—?"

Artemus nodded wordlessly and stepped forward, butterflies swarming his stomach. He could tell his brother and the other Guardians had sensed his tie with the stranger across their bond.

She met him halfway, her expression full of the same emotions storming through him.

"Hi," she murmured shakily.

Artemus raised a hand and caressed her cheek gently with his fingers. She shivered and closed her eyes, her body automatically turning into his touch. Desire blazed from the blue depths when she opened them once more.

"My name is—"

Artemus clasped her face and kissed her. She gasped and stiffened before melting in his arms, her mouth parting and her hands rising to cling to him as passionately as he held her. Artemus gently folded his wings around them, shielding them from curious eyes.

This meeting. This moment. This kiss.

It was theirs and theirs alone.

How long they embraced, Artemus didn't know. In that timeless spell, a thousand thoughts and memories rushed through his mind from the woman he loved, as well as a deeper understanding of the divine power that thrummed through her soul and the souls of her companions.

Someone cleared their throat discreetly.

Artemus reluctantly broke the kiss and pressed his forehead against his soulmate's, their skin so hot it was a miracle they hadn't scalded one another.

"Lily," he whispered against her lips, her name resonating through his consciousness.

She smiled tremulously and gripped his fingers tightly where they lay against her skin. "Hello, Artemus."

"You guys still kissing in there?" someone said impatiently.

A woman groaned. "Shut up, Will."

Artemus lowered his wings and studied the group of men and women behind Lily.

"I mean, I'm only asking for poor Tomas here," a guy with brown hair and blue eyes continued, cocking a thumb at another man with dark hair, green eyes, and a frown. "He looks like he's about to have a heart—*ouch!* What was that for?"

He scowled at Conrad Greene and rubbed the back of his head.

"Stop being an ass, son," Greene muttered.

"Artemus, this is Tomas." Lily indicated the man with the green eyes with a smile. "My brother."

"Hi," Tomas said with a grave nod.

"Hey," Artemus murmured.

Tomas looked past him. "Nate. Serena. It's good to see you again."

The super soldiers nodded hesitantly, their faces full of shock still.

"It's good to see you too," Serena mumbled. She stared at the men and women with him. "All of you."

Alexa King and Zachary Jackson smiled.

A little girl with ash-colored hair and blue eyes slipped out from behind a blonde with a gentle, wise smile. She darted past Artemus and Lily, walked brazenly up to the line of Guardians, and stopped in front of Jacob where he stood in his human form once more. She studied him with a focused expression before tugging on his hand and rising on her tiptoes.

Jacob gasped as the little girl pressed a firm kiss on his cheek.

"Mine," she declared with an assertive nod and a beaming grin.

Jacob paled. Callie gaped.

"You go, kid," Lou muttered to a stunned Jacob.

The man with brown hair, steel-blue eyes, and a pentagram on the back of his left hand standing next to the little girl's mother choked slightly on his breath. "Amelia!"

"Oh wow," Will said. "I think Uncle Ethan's gonna faint."

A tall, brawny man with a beard patted the little girl's father on the shoulder. "You'll get over it. Besides, Olivia has already given them her blessing."

"I don't want to get over it, Asgard," Pentagram Guy mumbled. He turned to the blonde at his side, his expression faintly accusing. "She's our precious daughter!"

She patted his cheek lightly. "We'll have to let her go at some point, honey."

A young woman the spitting image of Alexa King frowned at Lily. "So, who do I end up with?" She indicated the Guardians behind Artemus with an impatient wave of her hand. "You and Tomas have long hinted that one of these guys is my soulmate, so who is it?"

Sebastian frowned. "Soulmate?"

Artemus bit his lip, hearing Lily's mischievous chuckle in his mind. "I'll tell you later."

"Guess," Lily drawled.

The woman scowled. She pursed her lips and studied the wary Guardians.

"Well, it's not that guy." She pointed at Drake. "Super soldier chick looks like she'll claw my eyes out if I so much as smile at him."

Serena stepped closer to Drake.

The woman's gaze landed on Sebastian. "It's *definitely*

not that guy. He looks like he has a leather fetish and I'm not into that kind of kink."

"I object to that baseless accusation!" Sebastian protested.

"Let's see. Dragon guy has already been claimed. Amelia practically branded the kid as hers. That one's a priest. So that leaves—" The woman stiffened before glaring at Lily. "Wait! You're telling me I end up with the shop assistant?!"

She pointed an accusing finger at Otis.

Otis gaped.

Tomas sighed. "He's the seraph, Mila. He's probably the strongest guy among them."

Mila squinted, unconvinced. "He looks like a geek."

Otis frowned.

A teenage boy with dark hair and blue eyes smirked. "Mom married the biggest geek on the planet—*hey!*"

He glared at King and gingerly rubbed the spot on his head where she had slapped him.

"I can't believe I gave birth to this idiot," King told a grinning Jackson with an exasperated sigh.

Motion in the distance drew Artemus's gaze. A couple was approaching.

"Oh." Lily brightened. "They are here."

Artemus felt the love and adoration in her voice and across the bond that linked them as soulmates. He didn't need anyone to tell him that the man walking toward them was powerful. He could sense it with the stranger's every step and in his calm aura.

The woman with him stopped next to King and Greene, her eyes twinkling warmly.

"Artemus, these are my parents," Lily said.

The man stepped forward, his dark hair identical to his son's while his blue eyes shone with the same quiet strength as his daughter's.

He put his hand out. "Hi."

Artemus clasped it with a firm grip, the divine energy of the archangel who had given rise to the Immortal races dancing brightly against his own heavenly powers. In that moment, he sensed everything this man had experienced in his long and incredible life and saw a glimpse of the astounding destiny that still awaited them. A destiny they had been born to share and that would shape the future of mankind and of Heaven itself.

The man smiled, his expression telling Artemus he already knew of the extraordinary fate that linked them.

"My name is Lucas Soul."

THE END

AFTERWORD

To all my friends who helped make this possible. You know who you are.

To you, my readers. Thank you for reading Legion. I wrote this series because you wanted more stories in the Seventeen Universe. Legion delivered that, in spades. The next spin-off series in the Seventeen Universe kicks off late 2021. You can join my mailing list and/or my Facebook Group to find out more.

If you enjoyed my book, please consider leaving a review on Amazon or Goodreads. Reviews help readers like you find my books and I truly appreciate your honest opinions about my stories.

Want to know who Lucas Soul is? Turn the page to read an extract from Hunted, Lucas's story and the book that kickstarted the Seventeen Universe.

HUNTED EXTRACT

PROLOGUE

My name is Lucas Soul.

Today, I died again.

This is my fifteenth death in the last four hundred and fifty years.

~

CHAPTER ONE

I woke up in a dark alley behind a building.

Autumn rain plummeted from an angry sky, washing the narrow, walled corridor I lay in with shades of gray. It dripped from the metal rungs of the fire escape above my head and slithered down dirty, barren walls, forming puddles under the garbage dumpsters by my feet. It gurgled in gutters and rushed in storm drains off the main avenue behind me.

It also cleansed away the blood beneath my body.

For once, I was grateful for the downpour; I did not want any evidence left of my recent demise.

I blinked at the drops that struck my face and slowly climbed to my feet. Unbidden, my fingers rose to trace the cut in my chest; the blade had missed the birthmark on my skin by less than an inch.

I turned and studied the tower behind me. I was not sure what I was expecting to see. A face peering over the edge of the glass and brick structure. An avenging figure drifting down in the rainfall, a bloodied sword in its hands and a crazy smile in its eyes. A flock of silent crows come to take my unearthly body to its final resting place.

Bar the heavenly deluge, the skyline was fortunately empty.

I pulled my cell phone out of my jeans and stared at it. It was smashed to pieces. I sighed. I could hardly blame the makers of the device. They had probably never tested it from the rooftop of a twelve-storey building. As for me, the bruises would start to fade by tomorrow.

It would take another day for the wound in my chest to heal completely.

I glanced at the sky again before walking out of the alley. An empty phone booth stood at the intersection to my right. I strolled toward it and closed the rickety door behind me. A shiver wracked my body while I dialed a number. Steam soon fogged up the glass wall before me.

There was a soft click after the fifth ring.

'Yo,' said a tired voice.

'Yo yourself,' I said.

A yawn traveled down the line. 'What's up?'

'I need a ride. And a new phone.'

There was a short silence. 'It's four o'clock in the morning.' The voice had gone blank.

'I know,' I said in the same tone.

The sigh at the other end was audible above the pounding of the rain on the metal roof of the booth. 'Where are you?'

'Corner of Cambridge and Staniford.'

Fifteen minutes later, a battered, tan Chevrolet Monte Carlo pulled up next to the phone box. The passenger door opened.

'Get in,' said the figure behind the wheel.

I crossed the sidewalk and climbed in the seat. Water dripped onto the leather cover and formed a puddle by my feet. There was a disgruntled mutter from my left. I looked at the man beside me.

Reid Hasley was my business partner and friend. Together, we co-owned the Hasley and Soul Agency. We were private investigators, of sorts. Reid certainly qualified as one, being a former Marine and cop. I, on the other hand, had been neither.

'You look like hell,' said Reid as he maneuvered the car into almost nonexistent traffic. He took something from his raincoat and tossed it across to me. It was a new cell.

I raised my eyebrows. 'That was fast.'

He grunted indistinct words and lit a cigarette. 'What happened?' An orange glow flared into life as he inhaled, casting shadows under his brow and across his nose.

I transferred the data card from the broken phone into the new one and frowned at the bands of smoke drifting toward me. 'That's going to kill you one day.'

'Just answer the question,' he retorted.

I looked away from his intense gaze and contemplated

the dark tower at the end of the avenue. 'I met up with our new client.'

'And?' said Reid.

'He wasn't happy to see me.'

Something in my voice made him stiffen. 'How unhappy are we talking here?'

I sighed. 'Well, he stuck a sword through my heart and pushed me off the top of the Cramer building. I'd say he was pretty pissed.'

Silence followed my words. 'That's not good,' said Reid finally.

'No.'

'It means we're not gonna get the money,' he added.

'I'm fine by the way. Thanks for asking,' I said.

He shot a hard glance at me. 'We need the cash.'

Unpalatable as the statement was, it was also regrettably true. Small PI firms like ours had just about managed before the recession. Nowadays, people had more to worry about than what their cheating spouses were up to. Although embezzlement cases were up by a third, the victims of such scams were usually too hard up to afford the services of a good detective agency. As a result, the rent on our office space was overdue by a month.

Mrs. Trelawney, our landlady, was not pleased about this; at five-foot two and weighing just over two hundred pounds, the woman had the ability to make us quake in our boots. This had less to do with her size than the fact that she made the best angel cakes in the city. She gave them out to her tenants when they paid the rent on time. A month without angel cakes was making us twitchy.

'I think we might still get the cakes if you flash your eyes at her,' mused my partner.

I stared at him. 'Are you pimping me out?'

'No. You'd be a tough sell,' he retorted as the car splashed along the empty streets of the city. He glanced at me. 'This makes it what, your fourteenth death?'

'Fifteenth.'

His eyebrows rose. 'Huh. So, two more to go.'

I nodded mutely. In many ways, I was glad Hasley had entered my unnatural life, despite the fact that it happened in such a dramatic fashion. It was ten years ago this summer.

Hasley was a detective in the Boston PD Homicide Unit at the time. One hot Friday afternoon in August, he and his partner of three years found themselves on the trail of a murder suspect, a Latino man by the name of Burt Suarez. Suarez worked the toll bridge northeast of the city and had no priors. Described by his neighbors and friends as a gentle giant who cherished his wife, was kind to children and animals, and even attended Sunday service, the guy did not have so much as a speeding ticket to his name. That day, the giant snapped and went on a killing spree after walking in on his wife and his brother in the marital bed. He shot Hasley's partner, two uniformed cops, and the neighbor's dog, before fleeing toward the river.

Unfortunately, I got in his way.

In my defense, I had not been myself for most of that month, having recently lost someone who had been a friend for more than a hundred years. In short, I was drunk.

On that scorching summer's day, Burt Suarez achieved something no other human, or non-human for that matter, had managed before or since.

He shot me in the head.

Sadly, he did not get to savor this feat, as he died minutes after he fired a round through my skull. Hasley still swore to this day that Suarez's death had more to do with seeing me rise to my feet Lazarus-like again than the gunshot wound he himself inflicted on the man with his Glock 19.

That had been my fourteenth death. Shortly after witnessing my unholy resurrection, Hasley quit his job as a detective and became my business partner.

Over the decade that followed, we trailed unfaithful spouses, found missing persons, performed employee checks for high profile investment banks, took on surveillance work for attorneys and insurance companies, served process to disgruntled defendants, and even rescued the odd kidnapped pet. Hasley knew more about me than anyone else in the city.

He still carried the Glock.

'Why did he kill you?' said Reid presently. He braked at a set of red lights. 'Did you do something to piss him off?' There was a trace of suspicion in his tone. The lights turned green.

'Well, broadly speaking, he seemed opposed to my existence.' The rhythmic swishing of the windscreen wipers and the dull hiss of rubber rolling across wet asphalt were the only sounds that broke the ensuing lull. 'He called me an ancient abomination that should be sent straight to Hell and beyond.' I grimaced. 'Frankly, I thought that was a bit ironic coming from someone who's probably not that much older than me.'

Reid crushed the cigarette butt in the ashtray and narrowed his eyes. 'You mean, he's one of you?'

I hesitated before nodding once. 'Yes.'

Over the years, as I came to know and trust him, I told Reid a little bit about my origins.

I was born in Europe in the middle of the sixteenth century, when the Renaissance was at its peak. My father came from a line of beings known as the Crovirs, while my mother was a descendant of a group called the Bastians. They are the only races of immortals on Earth.

Throughout most of the history of man, the Crovirs and the Bastians have waged a bitter and brutal war against one another. Although enough blood has been shed over the millennia to fill a respectable portion of the Caspian Sea, this unholy battle between immortals has, for the most, remained a well-kept secret from the eyes of ordinary humans, despite the fact that they have been used as pawns in some of its most epic chapters.

The conflict suffered a severe and unprecedented setback in the fourteenth century, when the numbers of both races dwindled rapidly and dramatically; while the Black Death scourged Europe and Asia, killing millions of humans, the lesser-known Red Death shortened the lives of countless immortals. It was several decades before the full extent of the devastation was realized, for the plague had brought with it an unexpected and horrifying complication.

The greater part of those who survived became infertile.

This struck another blow to both sides and, henceforth, an uneasy truce was established. Although the odd incident still happened between embittered members of each race, the fragile peace has, surprisingly, lasted to this day. From that time on, the arrival of an immortal child into the world became an event that was celebrated at the highest levels of each society.

My birth was a notable exception. The union between a Crovir and a Bastian was considered an unforgivable sin and strictly forbidden by both races; ancient and immutable, it was a fact enshrined into the very doctrines and origins of our species. Any offspring of such a coupling was thus deemed an abomination unto all and sentenced to death from the very moment they were conceived. I was not the first half-breed, both races having secretly mated with each other in the past. However, the two immortal societies wanted me to be the last. Fearing for my existence, my parents fled and took me into hiding.

For a while, our life was good. We were far from rich and dwelled in a remote cabin deep in the forest, where we lived off the land, hunting, fishing, and even growing our own food. Twice a year, my father ventured down the mountain to the nearest village, where he traded fur for oil and other rare goods. We were happy and I never wanted for anything.

It was another decade before the Hunters finally tracked us down. That was when I learned one of the most important lessons about immortals.

We can only survive up to sixteen deaths.

Having perished seven times before, my father died after ten deaths at the hands of the Hunters. He fought until the very last breath left his body. I watched them kill my mother seventeen times.

I should have died that day. I did, in fact, suffer my very first death. Moments after the act, I awoke on the snow-covered ground, tears cooling on my face and my blood staining the whiteness around me. Fingers clenching convulsively around the wooden practice sword my father had given me, I waited helplessly for a blade to sink into my heart once more. Minutes passed before I realized I was alone in that crimson-colored clearing, high up in the Carpathian Mountains.

The crows came next, silent flocks that descended from the gray winter skies and covered the bloodied bodies next to me. When the birds left, the remains of my parents had disappeared as well. All that was left was ash.

It was much later that another immortal imparted to me the theory behind the seventeen deaths. Each one apparently took away a piece of our soul. Unlike our bodies, our souls could not regenerate after a death. Thus, Death as an ultimate end was unavoidable. And then the crows come for most of us.

No one was really clear as to where the birds took our earthly remains.

'What if you lived alone, on a desert island or something, and never met anyone? You could presumably never die,' Reid had argued with his customary logic when I told him this.

'True. However, death by boredom is greatly underestimated,' I replied. 'Besides, someone like you is bound to kill himself after a day without a smoke.'

'So the meeting was a trap?' said Reid.

His voice jolted me back to the present. The car had pulled up in front of my apartment block. The road ahead was deserted.

'Yes.' Rain drummed the roof of the Monte Carlo. The sound reminded me of the ricochets of machine guns. Unpleasant memories rose to the surface of my mind. I suppressed them firmly.

'Will he try to kill you again?' said Reid. I remained silent. He stared at me. 'What are you gonna do?'

I shifted on the leather seat and reached for the door handle. 'Well, seeing as you're likely to drag me back from Hell if I leave you high and dry, I should probably kill him first.'

I exited the car, crossed the sidewalk, and entered the lobby of the building. I turned to watch the taillights of the Chevrolet disappear in the downpour before getting in the lift. Under normal circumstances, I would have taken the stairs to the tenth floor. Dying, I felt, was a justifiable reason to take things easy for the rest of the night.

My apartment was blessedly cool and devoid of immortals hell-bent on carving another hole in my heart. I took a shower, dressed the wound on my chest, and went to bed.

Get Hunted now!

ABOUT A.D. STARRLING

Want to know about AD Starrling's upcoming releases?
Sign up to her newsletter for new release alerts, sneak
peeks, giveaways, and get a free boxset and exclusive
freebies.

Join AD's reader group on Facebook:
The Seventeen Club

Like AD's Author Page

Check out AD's website for extras and more:
www.adstarrling.com

BOOKS BY A.D. STARRLING

SEVENTEEN NOVELS

Hunted - 1

Warrior - 2

Empire - 3

Legacy - 4

Origins - 5

Destiny - 6

SEVENTEEN NOVEL BOXSETS

The Seventeen Collection 1 - Books 1-3

The Seventeen Collection 2 - Books 4-6

SEVENTEEN SHORT STORIES

First Death - 1

Dancing Blades - 2

The Meeting - 3

The Warrior Monk - 4

The Hunger - 5

The Bank Job - 6

The Seventeen Series Short Story Collection 1 (#1-3)

The Seventeen Series Short Story Collection 2 (#4-6)

The Seventeen Series Ultimate Short Story Collection (#1-6)

LEGION

Blood and Bones - 1

Fire and Earth - 2

Awakening - 3

Forsaken - 4

Hallowed Ground - 5

Heir - 6

Legion - 7

WITCH QUEEN

Coming soon

DIVISION EIGHT

MISCELLANEOUS

AUDIOBOOKS

Go to Authors Direct for a range of options where you can get AD's audiobooks.

CPSIA information can be obtained
at www.ICGtesting.com
Printed in the USA
LVHW090504050521
686547LV00040B/2080/J

9 781912 834198